THE GIRL WHO SINNED

BY THE SAME AUTHOR

It Must Have Been Love

THE GIRL WHO SINNED

JIGAR PRAJAPATI

Srishti
Publishers & Distributors

Srishti Publishers & Distributors
A unit of AJR Publishing LLP
212A, Peacock Lane
Shahpur Jat, New Delhi – 110 049

editorial@srishtipublishers.com

First published by
Srishti Publishers & Distributors in 2024

10 9 8 7 6 5 4 3 2 1

Printed and bound in India

ACKNOWLEDGEMENTS

I would like to express my deepest gratitude to all those who have supported and guided me throughout the creation of this book. Without your encouragement and assistance, this would not have been possible.

I am immensely grateful to my family and friends for their endless patience and understanding. Your unwavering love and support have provided me with the strength and motivation I needed to see this project to completion. Your belief in me was a constant source of inspiration.

A special thanks to the entire team at Srishti Publishers & Distributors, whose hard work and professionalism ensured that this book became a reality. Your dedication to excellence in every aspect of the publishing process, from design to marketing, has been truly remarkable.

To everyone who believed in me and my work, I am deeply thankful. I am honoured to have had the opportunity to work with such a talented and dedicated group of individuals.

THE BEGINNING

"Why are you always late, yaar? Can't you get ready on time just for once?"

Mona, my dear wife, was testing my patience. She always took so much time to get ready that we always ended up being late. We had to attend a far-off relative's wedding, and here we were running late. Again!

"It's all because of you," she blamed me as she hurriedly combed her hair.

"Excuse me! How am I to blame?"

"You should have woken me up earlier."

"That's not fair. I woke up after you and look at me… I'm ready and you're not."

"But you look extremely handsome today and I have to be at par with you." She winked at me and picked up her purse. "Let's go, hubby."

It was impossible to stay mad at her. She looked ravishing in her red sari. My jaw dropped as she stepped out. She came close and closed my mouth.

"Now I think it is you who is making us late."

I snapped out of my daze and followed her. My brother Sachin and his wife were ready and waiting for us.

I got into the driver's seat.

"We have to make a stop at Anand," Sachin said as we drove out of the house. Sachin used to visit Anand frequently as he donated money to a needy household every few months.

"I have never been there. You have to give me the directions,"

I said and after a few minutes of silence I asked, "So where are we going exactly?"

"To Rajan baa's house. You know about her, right? I had mentioned her plight to you."

"I have heard about her from you. But didn't she pass away a few years back?"

"Ya, she did. But her son is still alive. He is being taken care of by his daughter."

"Rajan baa had four granddaughters, didn't she?" Miral, Sachin's wife, questioned.

"OMG! Four granddaughters?" Mona was surprised.

"Ya, apparently the parents wanted a son, and they kept on trying in vain."

"Such a regressive mentality. Why are we wasting our money on such a family?" I asked.

"Absolutely right. Even though I had similar thoughts, those four girls were so sweet and talented, I thought the money would be put to good use. Earlier, the money was given to the four daughters to help with their education. Now all of them are married except one. She is the one taking care of her dad. I guess she needs the money to take care of her father."

"You said earlier that her dad never earned nor took proper care of them, so why is she taking care of her dad?" Miral questioned with a frown.

"Well, I suppose it's her innate kindness. He is her father, after all. Misty did not get married so that she could take care of him. Her three sisters send her money so that she doesn't have to work," Sachin elucidated.

"If her sisters are helping her run the house, then why do you need to give them anything? She must be getting a handsome amount," Mona said.

"Her sisters are not earning much. In fact, they are struggling to run their own households. The hospital charges are high. You know how much we had to pay when Mom was hospitalised. And if you guys have any problem, then you can tell me and I'll stop donating."

"No bhai, why would we have any problem? We've been together for more than forty years and whatever you have done is always right. We trust you. We just wanted to know about the family," I said as Sachin gave me directions to the house.

We arrived at an old single-storeyed house. It was dilapidated, with the paint peeling off the walls. The walls had visible cracks and water from leaking pipes was trickling down. It clearly needed renovation. The wooden windows seemed to be falling off their hinges. Many window panes were missing, and the gaps were covered with newspaper that had yellowed with age.

We got out of the car, and except for Sachin, we all looked at each other. The main gate was rusted with age. Sachin had to give it a good push before it finally opened, making a loud groaning sound. Hearing the loud screeching, somebody opened the main door which looked like it would fall apart at any moment. A beautiful lady opened the door. Her face lit up with a smile as she recognized Sachin.

"Arrey Sachin bhai? What a pleasant surprise. You should have informed me. Please come in."

The happiness was clearly visible in her eyes. She must be Misty, the daughter that Sachin had mentioned. She was charming, but her clothes were shabby and had clearly seen better days. She was trying to hide the stains on her clothes with her dupatta, but in vain. However, her smile made up for everything as she ushered us in.

An old man in tattered clothes was lying on a bed. He looked at Sachin and recognised him. He welcomed us with folded hands and a weak smile. Misty offered us a place to sit. I looked at the single bed which they used as a sofa. It was covered with an old stained bedsheet. Sachin, Miral, Mona and I sat down gingerly.

"So, what would you guys like to have?" Misty offered.

"Nothing, just sit with us and tell me how are your sisters?" Sachin asked.

"They are managing everything." She sounded a bit low.

"Is there any problem?" Sachin asked again.

"Well, it's that case against—"

Her father cut her short. "Misty, don't share our personal problems with outsiders. Please go and make some coffee for everyone."

I didn't like the manner in which he spoke to her. I sat and watched them quietly.

"No worries. I just came here to give you some money, nothing else. It'll come of some use," Bhai said, ignoring her father's words and offering her the envelope.

Misty eyes filled up with tears as she accepted the money with trembling hands. The reluctance was clearly visible on her face.

"We are really lucky to have a person like you in our life…"

Before she could finish her sentence, four children came running into the room. Noticing us, they stopped suddenly and started making silly faces at us.

"Oh my god, who are these cuties?" I asked.

"They are my sister's children. They had come here for their vacation. I wanted to spend some time with them. But their vacation is over and they are leaving in an hour," Misty said.

"They are so adorable!" Miral said.

"Don't be fooled by their faces; they are all terribly mischievous," Misty said. Mona took out some chocolates from her purse and offered them to the children.

"One by one, one by one," Misty said, but they paid no heed to her. They bolted towards Mona and jumped over her to get the chocolates. In all the excitement, the heaviest among them fell over Mona's leg. She screamed in pain as she tried to get her leg out from under him. The child, frightened out of his wits, immediately moved away.

Mona was in tears and could not move her leg. It seemed like a serious injury. Sachin and I rushed Mona to the car as I was certain it was a fracture. Misty started crying at the turn of events. Sachin went back and consoled her.

"It wasn't your fault at all," Sachin said. "It was an accident."

"I think we should take her to the hospital immediately," Miral said, observing Mona's pain. Sachin agreed, and we took her to the nearby hospital. Strangely, there were dozens of security personnel outside the hospital, much more than usual. But our focus was on Mona. We took her straight into the emergency ward and she was taken to be examined by a doctor. As she was being diagnosed, I got a call. It was a landline number. I picked up the call.

"Hello, this call is from the chief minister's office. Our CM wants to meet you," a man's voice said.

"I'm not in the mood for a joke. My wife is in the hospital, so whoever you are, just go to hell!"

I was furious and disconnected the call. In a few seconds, a doctor came out and informed us that Mona had to undergo a minor surgery. Sachin, being a doctor, agreed with the course of action.

"Everything will be fine," Sachin said.

"Why the hell do you want to help people? If it weren't for you, we wouldn't have come here," I lashed out at him.

"Calm down. It wasn't my fault. And you have seen her family. They really do need our help," he said.

"Don't you get that this was a sign from God? God doesn't want us to help that bloody family. We helped them and look at the result – Mona has to have a surgery."

"Okay, okay I get it. I won't go there again if you don't want me to," he said.

"I mean it."

"I know you are angry right now, so let's forget that for the time being."

He smiled sadly and started walking away.

I threw my hands up in resignation. "Sorry, I was furious. I know that the family is really poor and we should help them, but this was avoidable."

He stopped and turned back.

"No worries, just take care of her. I'll come back after dropping Miral home."

"No, don't worry about Mona. I'm here. You and Miral must go to the wedding. Do stay on for a couple of days and don't change the plan. I'm here to take care of Mona," I reassured him.

"Are you sure?" he asked, and I nodded my head.

Sachin left to join Miral. I went back to Mona and helped her to get ready for the OT. I was waiting outside when somebody tapped my shoulder.

"Rajiv? How did you know that I'm here?" I was surprised to see my cousin there.

"I didn't know you were here. By the way, why are you here?" he asked me, equally surprised.

"You tell me first," I insisted.

"I'm a regular donor here," he affirmed.

"Really? Donating blood is really noble," I said, a little sceptical. Knowing him, it was hard to believe he would donate blood.

"Even I would like to donate," I said, looking at him intently.

"Blood donation? Never, I hate needles," he said.

"Then what?"

A few seconds of silence later, it struck me. "Oh! Do you mean like Vicky Donor? I... I got it. What else could one expect from you?"

"Bhai..." He tried to come close to me and keep his hand on my shoulder, but I stopped him and said, "Have you washed your hands?"

He nodded his head, but I took a step back, keeping him at arm's length.

"If you're thinking about donating as well, they have good magazines to help you."

"Just shut up, yaar! You are in your forties now, and what are you doing?"

"Age is just a number, bro. Okay, I won't donate anymore. Anyway, you haven't told me what you are doing here?"

"You are a moron. I'm not telling you to stop donating. You are helping someone in need. And to answer your question, Mona injured her leg. We were close by so we brought her here."

This was not enough for him, so I shared the entire story with him.

"Oh! How is she now?"

"She is being operated on as we speak. Hoping for the best," I answered. As soon as I finished, I saw the doctor coming out of the OT.

"How is she?" I asked the doctor.

The doctor removed her gloves, facemask, and cap. She was a smart and suave lady. This was not lost on Rajiv. His eyes widened and there appeared a smile on his face. The doctor ignored him and said, "She's fine. She'll be transferred to a room where you can meet her."

She went back to her cabin, leaving Rajiv staring at her retreating back.

"She's just too good, man. Let's go and meet her," he said, looking in the direction of the doctor's cabin.

"I'm not going anywhere with you, and that's clear. I'm off to be with Mona."

"She said that you can meet her after she's shifted to a room. Not now," he protested.

"No means no."

"I'm still unmarried. She might be the one for me."

"Go to hell! I won't come with you."

I started walking towards the room and he started following me. Suddenly, he let out a shrill scream. I looked back, and he was lying on the floor. I bolted towards him. He was holding his right leg tightly and was screaming in pain. A few nurses rushed to our aid. We bolstered him to stand. I took one arm and put it on my shoulder to give him better support. We managed to take him to the doctor and put him down on a chair.

"So, where's the pain?" the doctor asked. I watched him point to his left leg and put it forward. I realized what he was up to. He was truly incorrigible. I stood up to leave the room.

"Please stay with me, Bhai. I can't bear the pain!" he moaned. I was in a fix. I had brought him in, so I had to stay. He turned to the doctor and continued, "My entire leg hurts."

"No, I mean, where does it hurt the most? Show me the exact point," she asked. She started moving her hand over his leg and every time she pressed his leg with her thumbs, he'd let out a scream. I could clearly see that he was just having a good time making a fool of the doctor.

"Get up!" the doctor said, looking at him sternly.

"I can't. Can't you see the pain I'm in? I need support to stand."

"I'll help you," I said.

"No, you can't do that by yourself. She has to help me as well," he said, looking at the doctor. I was very embarrassed and couldn't wait to give him a piece of my mind.

"Just get out of my cabin!" the doctor cried out in anger.

"But why?" Rajiv said, pretending to be bewildered.

"Get out or I'll operate on all your three legs," she lashed out.

"Sorry to interrupt, but he has only two," I interrupted.

"You know which third leg I'm talking about. The pain in the phantom leg? You were screaming wherever I pressed. Don't you understand that you are sitting in front of a doctor? At least think before you speak or act. And let me tell you that you are the worst actor ever!"

Then she turned to me. "Don't you feel ashamed? To be a part of all this drama while your wife is recovering. Now don't waste my time and get out, otherwise I'll have to call the staff," she said.

I was already heading towards the door, livid at Rajiv's

behaviour. But Rajiv didn't budge and instead settled comfortably into his chair.

"Quite intelligent, I like you," Rajiv started. I couldn't believe it. Had he lost his mind?

"Should I get the sandals out or will a syringe work?"

The doctor took a syringe lying on the table. Rajiv stared at her for a few seconds. He quickly picked up a pen lying on the table and started writing something on a piece of paper.

"So, this is my contact number. You can call me when you're free."

She stood up with both her hands on the table and was about to say something, but I stopped her and took Rajiv out by force.

"Are you mad? What were you doing?" I screamed at him.

"You all say that I should get married, but whenever I try to get to know a girl, you guys stop me. I've reached my forties and am still unmarried just because of people like you in my life. Anyway, I know you can't bear to see me happy. Just take care of Mona. I know that the doctor will call me back. You just wait and watch," he said and left.

What a weirdo, I thought as I watched him leave. I returned my attention to Mona after this slight digression. She was hardly conscious when I reached. She had a little glimpse of me and went back to sleep.

"Hey, do you want some water? How are you feeling?" I asked after she woke up.

"If you'll remove your hand from my leg, then it'll be less painful," she said. I removed my hand with an apologetic smile. I recounted my encounter with Rajiv and also mentioned the fake call from the CM's office.

"How did you know that it was a fake call?"

"Obviously. Why would she call me?"

"Arreey! How can you be so irresponsible? What if it was not fake?"

"It has to be. I know that. And even if she really needs me, she will call back again. Why don't you just rest for some time? I'll be back in a while."

I went out and pondered. Could it have been a genuine call? No, why would she call me? I had to be sure, so I decided to call the number.

"We knew that you'd call us back," said the same voice again.

"Okay, I'm sorry, but I wasn't really expecting a call from you. Still, I find it hard to believe that you are calling from the CM's office," I said.

"Well, how do we convince you? Hmmmm... Okay, let me tell you that right now you are in Sayajirao Hospital, where your wife is admitted."

I was dumbfounded. Now this was getting quite scary.

"What do you want?" I asked after a pause.

"Hope that was enough to make you believe that we are for real. And don't be worried. We won't do anything to your wife or your family. Our CM just wanted to meet you for some personal work," the man on the other side said.

I was excited and nervous. I was also rather flummoxed. Why me?

"Okay, where and when?"

"She is in the same hospital that you are in. In a few minutes, a person will come to you and take you to her. But let me tell you that no one knows that she is in Sayaji. So please let this remain confidential."

Before I could say anything, he hung up. I wondered why the hell our CM wanted to meet me. I turned around and found a black commando standing tall in front of me. I accidentally bumped into him and looked at his face. He was steady and strong like a rock and remained expressionless.

"Follow me," he said in a steely voice. I nodded and followed him blindly.

Why the hell was he taking me to Mona's room? I thought as I saw him stop in front of her room.

"I don't think that's the CM's room. You are going to the wrong room," I called out.

But he ignored me and opened the door. I entered the room and was shocked at the scene in front of me. Mona was surrounded by guards. The fear was apparent on her face.

"Don't be worried… they won't do anything to her," I heard someone say.

I looked around and found the CM sitting on the sofa.

"Maya Baldaniya…" I whispered in surprise. She had covered herself with a shawl. The veins of her hands were clearly visible. She didn't look healthy at all, but her aura was undiminished. Her face was bright as always. She sat upright with her legs crossed.

I said, "Sorry, ma'am, but I shouldn't have taken your name. Ma'am, we are extremely sorry if we've done something wrong. Please let us go."

I was drenched with sweat. I took my handkerchief and wiped my face. I tried to go close to her to plead my case, but the guards stopped me. What was going on?

"Okay, okay, I won't go. But please, ma'am, tell me what is the matter," I said earnestly. She remained poker-faced, then smirked.

"Have a seat," she said quietly and pointed to a single revolving chair. I obeyed. Her bangles made a captivating sound as she lifted her hand. All the bangles were mismatched. I watched her silently as she pointed to a guard and ordered him something in sign language. One of the guards pushed my chair closer to Maya Baldaniya. She leaned towards me.

"Listen, I'm not feeling well, so I will come straight to the point," she whispered. She took a deep breath and said, "*Ek murder karne ka hain*." (You have to commit a murder.) I couldn't believe what I had heard. I stood up from my chair, but the guard put his hands on my shoulders and pushed me down again.

"I know you're shocked, but I couldn't find a better candidate than you. I had sent a person this morning to kill him, but you were there so he couldn't do it. And while returning, he met with an accident. So now you have to complete the task as I couldn't find another person at such short notice," she said in a matter-of-fact manner.

There was complete silence for a few minutes. My hands were shaking, and I began perspiring profusely. I hadn't expected this from Mayaben. I looked at Mona with fear in my eyes.

Mayaben observed me and said, "Don't worry about what goes on in the hospital; we'll take care of your wife."

Fear was running through my veins. I wanted to speak, but words weren't coming out of my mouth.

"This is the address. Go and kill him," she said and handed me a chit of paper. She leaned back in her chair and stared at me.

"Please ma'am, you're mistaken. I haven't been to any place. I don't know who you are talking about. Please let me go," I pleaded.

She took out a gun and kept it on the table. She clearly meant business.

"Nothing to worry about. You just follow my instructions. You take care of me and I'll take care of your wife. Don't use your brain; leave that part to me."

I took a deep breath as I kept wiping away the tears that were rolling down my cheeks.

"Look, whoever you are, I'm not going to do this at any cost. You want to kill us both, just go ahead," I managed to say.

"Eh! Shekhar, get that bag here."

She ignored me and called one of her men with a bag. She opened up the bag, and it was all filled with money. I took the bag in my hand, zipped it and handed it back to her and said, "Thank you, but no. No means no."

It seemed like my anger didn't have any effect on her. She was still calm. She turned her eyes and indicated something to one of her guards. The man went to Mona and placed a knife on her neck. He covered her mouth with tape so that she couldn't cry out. I stood up to stop the man, but his aides rushed towards me and held me tightly. One covered my mouth with his hands. I could not move a step forward, nor could I make a sound. After a few seconds, I got tired of trying. Once I was calm, they let me go. I just said, "Just kill us both, but I won't do it."

After a few seconds of silence, Mayaben got up and came close to my ear and whispered, "What if I kill only one and send you to jail for killing your wife?"

I again tried to get out of the clasp of the men, but it was fruitless. Mayaben went back to her chair and nodded to the man who held Mona. The guy pressed the knife and a tiny trickle of blood appeared on Mona's neck. I shouted, "I'll do it… I'll do it. Just stop what you are doing!"

That man stopped. Mayaben gestured to the guards to let me go. She told me to look at the chit in my hand. I looked at it but didn't read it. I was in a daze. Why me?

"There's only one man in the house, so you won't need his photograph. Just go and do it."

I did not say anything and turned to leave.

"And listen, if you are thinking of involving the police, then let me tell you they are already involved," she said, leaning back in her chair.

This was followed by silence. I was thoroughly trapped. There was nothing I could do. I fiddled with my fingers and let out a sigh. I had to save Mona, so I was left with no choice but to do Mayaben's bidding.

I went out and looked down at the piece of paper. I hailed an autorickshaw to take me to the address. The driver took a very familiar route. And to my shock, the auto stopped right outside Misty's house. Her father was the only man there. But why the hell did Mayaben want me to kill her father? I was absolutely clueless. I opened the gate, forgetting the loud noise it made. Misty opened the main door almost instantly.

"Hey, did you leave anything behind? And how's Mona?" she asked, looking worried.

"She's fine. I think I left my handkerchief here. I was passing by so thought I'd collect it," I said in a steady voice.

"Is anything wrong? You seem to be worried." The stress was apparent on my face.

"No, but Mona had to undergo a surgery, so I was worried. But everything's fine now."

"Okay. Do come in. Would you like to have some water?"

"No, but I think I'll have some coffee if it is no trouble," I said to buy some time. "Where are the children?"

"I had told you in the morning that their vacation was over, so they left an hour ago. I'm really sorry that they hurt your wife. Do have a seat. I'll be back with some hot coffee."

After she left, I turned and saw that her father was still sleeping. I went close to him with a pillow in my hands. I had no weapon, nor did I have a plan. He was sleeping on his left side and I didn't know how to put the pillow on his face. Suddenly, he turned towards me and opened his eyes.

"What are you doing? Do you want to kill me?" he chided. I started sweating.

"A... ba... nothing. I just wanted to make sure that you're comfortable. I thought this pillow would be better for you. It's softer. I was just trying to change it without disturbing you."

He lifted his head up and said, "Put it there and go back to your place."

I changed the pillow under his head and went back. Misty came with a cup of coffee and handed it to me.

"So, did you find it?" she asked.

"What?" I was surprised.

"Handkerchief?"

"Oh! No, I couldn't find it. I must have dropped it somewhere else."

"You can finish your coffee. I have something to take care of. I just need a moment. I am so sorry."

I smiled politely. I had gotten another opportunity. I kept my coffee on the table and approached him with another pillow.

"Kya? I'm still awake. Just finish your coffee or else I'll kick you."

I smiled at him meekly and went back to my place. This wasn't going to be easy. I sipped the coffee and tried to calm my nerves. Misty's dad propped his head up on his hand so that he could see me clearly. He stared at me continuously, making me very uncomfortable. And why the hell was the coffee so hot? I gulped it down and smiled back at her father. Misty returned after finishing her work.

"How was the coffee?" she asked.

"He must have burnt his tongue. Why the hell did you waste so much milk to make coffee for him? Anyway, I need to go to the loo," he said and went inside.

"Misty, I know that it is not my business, but why are you taking care of this guy? I mean he never speaks well of you, nor does he treat you well. As Bhai said, he never took care of you and your sisters. Then why?" I asked.

She kept mum for a while.

I added, "Don't you think he should die?"

I realized that I shouldn't have said that, but it didn't seem to affect her.

"You're right. I don't consider him as my father. He isn't worthy of being called our father. But as Rajan baa had always taught us – to never lose our humanity. He is just another human and I'm taking care of him. If I'll do what he did to me, then what would be the difference between us?"

She sighed, "I think I know what I'm doing. You better leave now as I have a lot of work to do," she said and went inside.

She was so nice. What was I trying to do? To kill another to save my own. I couldn't do it, come what may. I took an auto and went back to the hospital.

I opened the door of the room and bolted towards Mona. I

removed the tape from her mouth and grabbed a knife lying on the table. I kept it on my wrist. Looking at Mayaben I said, "You want to kill only one, right? Just try to come near us and I'll kill myself. You don't understand what 'love' is but I do. That girl Misty does. She loves her dad irrespective of the kind of person he is and how he's treated her. But you don't have a heart. How would you know what love is?"

There was pin-drop silence. Mayaben looked at me.

"Please clear the room," she instructed her men in a steady voice. I thought it had worked. As the last of her guards closed the door behind him, she looked up. There were tears in her eyes though her face was devoid of any emotion.

"Love? Who else would know this word better than me? My dad did not want a girl child, so he told my mother to kill me in her womb. But she wanted me and kept me and fought for me."

"If you know what love is then why do you want to kill someone?"

"That's not 'someone.' That's my husband… my ex-husband," she said, sitting up straight.

That was a shocking revelation. Why did she want to kill him? And if that was her house then why was it in such a poor condition? My mind was flooded with questions.

She got up, removed her shawl and came close to us. She pulled up a chair close to Mona's bed. She held Mona's hand in hers and said,

"Love? I have fallen in love thrice. You would never find a woman as lucky as me."

As she spoke, she appeared to be lost in her thoughts. She suddenly became vulnerable. Mayaben, the formidable CM was replaced by a frail woman, whose withered face reflected countless emotions.

1

Maya

Her Story

My mother gave birth to me against my father's wishes. As I grew up, I became the cause of their endless fights. I never believed that he didn't love me at all. He did take care of me at times, but I led a very restricted life. I wasn't allowed much freedom. I loved watching movies and wanted to dress like the heroines I admired. But my dad hated that. He never allowed me to wear short clothes. I did understand that he was concerned for my safety, because during those times, wearing short clothes was taboo. But I was a young girl trying to break free from all the shackles. I loved swimming costumes, and I always wondered why I wasn't allowed to wear them.

"Ma, look at Helen. She is so beautiful. I love her outfits. Please get me a dress like hers," I pleaded with my mother.

"Are you out of your mind? Don't you know your dad? He'll kill us both."

"He wanted to kill me when I was not even born," I said.

"Yeah, you are right but that was before you were born. The day you were born, however, he said nothing. Maybe he accepted that you were his daughter no matter what," Ma was trying to make me understand. But I wasn't convinced.

"And what about his restrictions?"

"You consider them restrictions, but he considers them as protection."

"Protection my foot! You can't protect someone by putting restrictions on them."

"Put yourself in your father's shoes. Look at things from his point of view. Don't argue about everything," my mother tried to reason with me.

But I was in no mood to let go. It was a fight for my rights and I wasn't going to give in so easily.

I ignored my mother's warning. I went to a nearby shop to buy a dress like I had seen the actress wear in a movie. I found one and happily went back home with the bag in my hands. I tried on the pretty knee-length dress and went to Ma happily.

"What on earth are you wearing?" she said with a big frown on her face.

"How am I looking?" I said ignoring her tense face.

"Just go and change. We don't wear such clothes in our house. I might kill you before your dad does!" She was furious.

"I don't know why you are so worried. Look at the world and look at us. We seem to be stuck in the old days. It's time to move ahead. And I'm sure Papa is not going to react the way you think."

"I don't care about the world. My family is my world. And I care about the society and what they will say. Our reputation will be at stake," she said in anger.

Maybe she was right but at that age, it was quite difficult for me to understand her. I wanted to be a free bird. We argued for a few more minutes, till we heard the door open. It was my father. He stood at the door staring at me with piercing eyes. I was terrified and started sweating. Without saying a word, he walked over to Ma and slapped her.

"I don't think I need to tell you why I slapped you."

Mom's face was expressionless, and she looked at me, making me feel guilty.

"It wasn't her fault. In fact, she was telling me to change," I dared to enter their conversation.

Papa bolted towards me and slapped me so hard that I fell down a few feet away from him. "Don't you dare interrupt when we are talking."

He went back to Ma and hit her again. "You've given her the freedom to answer back. Teach her to stay within her limits."

He did not stop there. He went on beating her. A surge of anger swept through me. I got up, picked up a glass jar from the table, and brought it down on his head with all my strength. Blood trickled down his forehead as I remained with my hands in the air, trying to make sense of what I had done.

Ma gasped in horror and slapped me. She took the jar from my hand and threw it on the floor. She sat next to Papa and pressed the wound with the pallu of her saree.

"Just go and call an auto! Fast!" she screamed at me.

I rushed out in panic. He was seriously hurt. We got him to the hospital quickly. I knew that I could be jailed if he died. The next two days were critical as the doctors tried their best to treat him. Guilt was eating me alive, and I prayed that he would be okay. On the third day, we got the good news that he was out of danger, much to our relief. We took him home and nursed him back to health. One good thing that came out of that episode was that he never raised his voice at us again.

I began to take advantage of my newfound freedom and soon became the talk of the town. I was on cloud nine, enjoying all the attention. On Thursdays, the students in our school were allowed to wear clothes of their choice. I looked forward to the day and would be ready with a new outfit every week. I wanted everyone to take an interest in me and soon became the centre of attraction for every boy in our school except one – Nayan. He was a very decent guy. He was cool and sophisticated and was a topper like me.

"Why are you pretending that you don't have any interest in me?" I finally dared to ask him.

"Am I? I didn't realize that. However, it seems like you're taking quite an interest in me," he said and walked away.

The two toppers of the class had finally spoken to each other. His words kept ringing in my ears. Was it true? Was I really attracted to him? I brushed my thoughts aside and decided not to talk with him anymore.

I went to school as usual the next day. I sat on one of the benches at the back of the class. Nayan was sitting in the row in front of me. I was not able to concentrate on what the teacher was teaching. Every few seconds my eyes would turn towards Nayan. But he never looked back.

"Maya, stand up and please explain everything I said."

Our teacher was trying to get out of having to repeat what he had taught, so was asking a random student to repeat the lesson. Usually, I could always answer, but on that day, I drew a complete blank. I just stood up and remained mum.

"I didn't expect this from you, Maya."

Sir was furious and asked Nayan to explain. He explained everything without any hesitation. As he was speaking, I was filled with a warm, fuzzy feeling. It felt like no one else was in class except us. I got up from my seat and started walking towards him, my eyes on his face. His longish hair was being ruffled by the wind of the fan over him. I took a moment to observe his bright face with light pink lips, saying something beautiful in slow motion. His eyes were synchronising with his facial expressions.

"Maya, why are you not listening to me? I said go back to your seat!"

I snapped out of my daze. Oh god! What did I just do? Everyone was laughing at me. I started crying. What were these feelings that I had never felt before? I wasn't able to figure out the things happening to me. I decided to have a talk with Nayan during our recess. I didn't know why I was so attracted to him.

"Hi, can I?" I asked Nayan when he was sitting all alone in the school canteen.

"Ya, why not?"

He offered me the chair next to him. I sat down while he continued to have his food. He kind of didn't care about my presence. He was busy finishing the plate of dhokla in front of him. He didn't even glance up at me. Meanwhile, I was observing him intently. He was certainly making my heart beat faster. The world seemed to be in slow motion all of a sudden. I could smell him rather than those dhoklas. But who cared? I was being ignored, and that made me furious. I was waiting for him to say something but he was too busy devouring his food. I got up to leave.

"Wait, don't you want to say something?" He stopped me with those words. A smile returned to my face. I turned to him but he was still busy with his food. I realized that he'd just asked a question and nothing else.

"No, nothing I guess," I replied, waiting for his response.

He kept down his spoon and closed his dabba. He stood up and came closer to me. He brushed the strands of hair away from my face and kissed me. Right there in the canteen. The blood rushed through my veins. Time stood still for a moment. And I didn't want the moment to end. He then took his bag and left like nothing had happened.

I stood there in a trance as I watched his retreating back. I was trying to take in what had just happened. Whatever happened was very new for me; a kind of feeling that cannot be explained. I touched my lips and smiled like a madman.

"You look very happy today," Ma said, noticing my smiling face when I reached home.

"Ma, I got my first kiss," I whispered. I had to tell someone.

"Have you lost it? You are just sixteen years old. And think before you speak. I'm your mother," she said, shocked at my candid confession.

"I don't think you are only my mother. You are my best friend as well. You have always told me not to hide anything from you. If you don't want me to tell you such things, I won't." I kept my head on her warm lap.

"Never hide anything from me, my dear."

She held my face and made me look at her. She added, "I'm glad you consider me as a friend and not only a mother. But you have to be careful. Don't let your feelings get the better of you. I'm glad that you've found someone for yourself. But don't cross the limits."

I nestled in her lap again.

"Don't worry about that. I know my limits. And Nayan does as well. He's a good boy. I don't think he will force me to do anything I don't want to." I had a smile on my face.

"I trust you. And I would love to meet him. After that we will decide what to do," she said as she stroked my hair. After a short pause, she added,

"Beta, I want to say one more thing to you. You must limit your expenses. You know, after that incident, your father lost his job. He doesn't earn as much as he used to. Now, it is getting difficult to make ends meet."

"Okay Ma, I won't spend any money on dresses or makeup. From now onwards simplicity will be my style."

I was old enough to understand my family's financial problems. And I took care not to spend any money unnecessarily. The thing I learned was that your clothes don't make you, it is your attitude that makes up your personality.

Meanwhile, the whole school was talking about us. I started spending less time with my friends and more with Nayan. Earlier I would try to explain the definition of love and I couldn't. Then Nayan came into my life. He didn't explain anything about love, but for me, he was love itself. He was love personified. And I understood why nobody could define love, because it was a deep feeling and emotion, impossible to convey in words.

One of our favourite things to do together was watch movies in the theatre. We'd book the corner seats and watch any movie that was playing. It was the world's best feeling to hold his warm hand during the movie. We'd steal kisses in the darkness; his soft lips filled me with an indescribable warmth. Those were the best days of my life, filled with endless possibilities. I think we were the only couple in our school. Time flew by and two years passed by in the blink of an eye. We were still head over heels in love with one another, and it wasn't easy for us to control our emotions and feelings.

"Hey Maya, I need your help," Nayan came to me during break time one day at school. We were in our final year of high school.

"Ya, please say."

"I have some doubts I need to clarify in our maths syllabus. I know you are far better at mathematics than me. Will you help me?"

"I know that I'm the best," I retorted with a smile. "Okay tell me what are your doubts?"

"There are quite a few. I think you should come home. We can solve them together. Only if you are comfortable, of course. I really want us to top the class again."

"I don't mind if your parents don't have an issue."

"My parents are not home."

He held my hand and added, "Hope you don't have a problem with that. I swear we won't do anything other than studies," he promised.

"I believe you, Nayan. I know we can control our feelings. Let's go after our last class then."

We hailed an auto to go to Nayan's place. We hardly spoke during the drive. I was rather nervous. We were dropped in front of a huge iron gate. We could not see through it. Nayan went near the gate and knocked. Somebody from inside opened a small slit; he looked at Nayan and opened the gate. The guards were staring at us like we were going to do something wrong. I had a fake smile on my face and continuously adjusted my uniform.

A buggy car drove us to his house. I marvelled at the landscaping. The driveway had beautiful gardens on either side. The main garden in the centre as we approached the house was mesmerizing. It was designed to look like the human eye. At the centre was a huge fountain which contained a sculpture of three fishes with water flowing out of their mouths. There were flowers of every colour and the lawn was emerald green. The birds seemed to welcome us with their songs.

I held his hand in mine and said, "I did not know much about you. You are very wealthy."

We reached the palatial house. To enter the main door, we had to climb up a few steps made of white marble. We removed our shoes near the door and the coolness of the marble was pleasant on the soles of my feet.

Nayan rang the antique bell hanging in front of the door. A well-dressed maid opened the door and welcomed us. As soon as we entered the house she closed it and returned to her work.

"You have got such an amazing house! It's so big and beautiful. I would like to see the whole house first," I demanded.

"Of course, just follow me," he said and took me with him.

It was like the houses one saw in movies. The floors were made of white shining marble and the décor was exquisite. The curtains shimmered from huge bay windows. I could imagine the number of servants one needed to maintain the house.

"I have a question for you," I said.

"Please, go ahead."

"If you are so rich then why are you studying in a school like ours? I mean you can clearly afford to go to a much better school."

"My parents believe that the school doesn't play an important role in upbringing, as the parents' upbringing. So, they found a good school close to home so that they could spend maximum time with their child. Simple!"

"Wow, that's a novel thought. Now I think we should focus on your doubts. It's getting late," I insisted.

Nayan took me to his room. His bedroom was as large as my entire house. A four-poster bed stood in the middle. A study table with heavy wooden chairs was placed in the opposite corner. We took our seats at the study table. We started solving the problems one by one. Many times our hands touched accidentally, and a very strange feeling ran through my body.

There was a strange fear I was feeling, mingled with excitement. It was winter time and my heart was beating faster than usual. As our hands touched over the table, he caught mine. I pulled it away and continued with the lesson. He again took my hand in his intentionally.

"Please Nayan, we mustn't get distracted," I insisted.

He looked into my eyes, caught my other hand and said "I can't control myself."

I let my guard down and kissed his smooth lips. He kissed me back passionately and started playing with my long hair. He lifted me in his arms and brought me to his bed. Our bodies were pressed against each other. Everything was happening too fast. We didn't even realize that we were crossing the limits as we gave in to our desires.

"We shouldn't have done this," I said filled with guilt as we lay next to each other.

"Don't be worried. This was going to happen sooner or later."

"It wasn't the right time. You haven't talked to your parents yet. What if they don't accept our relationship?" I said. I was rather scared. I got up from the bed and put my clothes on.

"Don't get so tense. Everything will be fine," Nayan tried to reassure me.

"I think I should leave now. I need some time by myself."

I left the room, putting an end to our discussion. When I was entering the house, I didn't feel bad when the staff were staring at me. But I was more concerned on my way out about who was looking at me and in which way. And I was not wrong about them thinking the worst about me. I rushed out as quickly as possible and ran outside the bungalow. I was about to cry but controlled myself and caught an autorickshaw. I took a few deep breaths and calmed myself down. The fear and the hesitation lessened and were soon replaced by a sense of gratification. I made myself believe that Nayan wouldn't leave me. He would be my future. I reached home in a few minutes.

"Maya, why are you so late?" Ma asked.

"Had some work, Ma."

"Hope you are not doing anything wrong," she said as she placed my food before me.

Physically, I was at home but mentally I was still with Nayan. I was in a different zone and it seemed like proof that I had become an adult. I was in utopia and soon fell into a deep slumber.

It was a Thursday. I wanted to look especially pretty that day. It was a special day for me. I wanted Nayan's complete attention. I reached school a little late that day and was surprised to see that Nayan was late as well. In fact, he never showed up. I sat all alone. People around me were trying to talk to me, but I wasn't interested and was preoccupied.

'He must have reached late and the security must have not allowed him to enter,' I tried to reason with myself.

My thoughts didn't let me calm down. I was consumed by fear as negative thoughts began rushing into my head. I spent a miserable day at school, waiting for the last class. I couldn't attend a single lecture with proper concentration. My eyes were on the classroom door. I bolted home the minute school was over. Huffing and puffing, I picked up the landline and dialled his number.

"Hello, Nayan?" I managed to say. My lips were trembling and my hands were shaking.

"Sorry, ma'am, but Baba is not at home," the voice replied.

"Do you know where he is?" I asked.

"In school. He will be back in a few minutes. Why don't you do one thing? Call after ten minutes again."

I was shocked. He certainly wasn't in school. If not in school, where would he have gone? Maybe he had spent the day out so that his parents wouldn't get furious. Only he can answer all the questions. I was sure he'd call back. I waited for ten minutes before I called him again.

The same person picked up the phone.

"Hello, I'm Maya again. Is he back?" I asked him again.

"Oh yes, he's back, but he's gone to his room. I guess he's not feeling well. Please call back tomorrow," he said and hung up before I could say anything. There was no point in calling back. I'd have to wait for the next day. I was sure to meet him in school.

I woke up early the next morning and got ready for school. I was the first one to reach school with the hope of meeting Nayan as soon as he arrived. But to my surprise, he was absent again. Something was amiss. I was worried and felt terribly guilty. I wanted to beat myself. Why did I sleep with him? I felt cheated.

I dialled his number again after reaching home.

'This number is out of service', I heard the pre-recorded message. I was at my wit's end. I tried again, again and again. Finally, I threw the receiver in frustration and began crying. Ma ran out of the kitchen. She picked up the receiver lying on the floor and kept it back.

"What happened? Why is my child so angry?" she asked as she hugged me tightly.

"Ma, I'm sorry."

"Sorry for what beta? Have you fought with someone? Or has somebody said anything mean to you?"

"No, Ma… nothing like that. I'll be fine." I said, wiping off my tears, trying to compose myself. But she was my mother and she wouldn't leave and insisted I tell her the truth.

"I know there's something. Sharing your troubles will make you feel better."

"What do you want to know, Ma? That I slept with someone?" I burst out. It was a relief to say the words aloud.

"Ma, now he's not responding at all. I gave him my everything, assuming that he loved me and he would marry me. Ma, I should have stopped him. But I didn't," I sobbed.

"I had warned you earlier because I never wanted you to face such a situation. Now stop crying. Just accept whatever happened. We can't change the past but we should not allow it to change our future. Just move on."

"It's not that easy, I really liked him."

I was baffled with her reaction. I thought she'd throw me out of the house. Instead, she was supportive like a good friend.

"It is not very hard either. Forget him and concentrate on your studies. Now go to sleep."

She kept her hand on my head and then got up to leave.

"Ma, don't you think we should make a legal complaint against him?" I asked her. She stopped and turned back.

"Did he force you?"

"No," I replied after a pause of a few seconds. I looked into her eyes and realized that I couldn't blame Nayan. It had been consensual.

"Have a good night. And get ready for school tomorrow. And

don't you dare let him come into your dreams," she joked trying to lighten the situation and closed the door behind her.

When I reached school the next day, I wasn't surprised to see that he was absent. I soon found out that he had left the school altogether. I decided to close that chapter and began concentrating on my studies. But Nayan was my first love. It wasn't that easy to get rid of him. In other words, one can say God was not ready to let me move on so easily.

Our final exams were around the corner. I was busy studying hard and had even forgotten Nayan. It had been more than two months since I had last seen him. One evening, I was studying in my room. My throat felt parched, so I went to the kitchen for a glass of water. Suddenly, I felt dizzy and fell flat on the floor. When I woke up, I found that I was in a hospital. Ma was sitting right next to me while my father stood facing the window. He turned to me when he saw I was awake.

"What happened to me?"

"Nothing to worry about. We have to have a small operation and everything will be fine."

"That's okay, but tell me what's the problem?" I asked again.

"Why the hell don't you tell her what is wrong? You are pregnant, you stupid girl! You have ruined my name," Papa cried out in anger.

I froze for a minute as I let the words sink in. A baby… our baby? I understood what Ma meant by an operation. I became numb and then began to cry uncontrollably. Mom tried to console me and hugged me tightly.

"Everything will be fine, bachcha…"

"Ma, I don't want an abortion," I wiped my tears and said.

"Are you mad? Do you want us to live? Or do you want us to go and lie on a railway track?" Papa was tenser than I was.

"Let me talk to her," Ma interrupted and added.

"That's your choice as you are eighteen now. You can make your own decision; I won't force you. But if I was in your place, I would have gone ahead with the operation. You have your whole future ahead of you. Think carefully."

"You are right, Ma, but this is not only my child alone. Nayan should know about this."

Ma did not argue and it was decided that I should meet Nayan once before making a decision. Dad was furious but there was little he could do apart from hitting the wall with his fist. As soon as I was discharged from the hospital I went straight to Nayan's house. After knocking on the huge door for a while, a middle-aged man opened it. I guessed he was Nayan's father.

"Yes?"

"Uncle, is Nayan there?" I said hesitantly.

"You must be Maya, please come in. I was waiting for you. I was hoping you had forgotten about Nayan and had moved on. Anyway, just come in."

He ushered me to a sofa. As I looked around the grand sitting room, the memories of my first visit came flooding to my mind. I was as nervous as I had been that day, though for a very different reason.

"So, what's the matter? I'm his dad," the gentleman said.

"Uncle, it would be better if I meet him."

"Look, let me come directly to the point. First thing, he is not home now. Secondly, I don't like you being here. Sorry I'm being harsh, but it's a fact. I got to know from my servants that you had come home some months ago. The same day I talked to the principal of your school and got all your details. I gathered some info about your family background too."

He spoke without a pause. His words pierced my soul. Why the hell weren't my tears in my control? Why didn't they ask for permission before flowing?

He continued, "I knew that you guys were dating. And let me tell you it was all fun for Nayan. But I did not trust you, so I just changed his school. I did not want to tell you all this but now that you are here, let me be clear. You can come nowhere close to Nayan in terms of class or background. You think I don't know what you girls are after? You cannot fool us. A gold digger – that's what you are. I think you've got your answer, so it would be better if you leave," he said and got up from his chair.

"I haven't got the answer to the main question," I managed to say as I wiped my tears. "What about the child in my womb?"

"Child? Go to the father. Why have you come here? Nayan is not your only partner, I'm sure!"

I stood up in a daze. I had never felt so insulted in my life. My ears were ringing with his words. I calmly walked out of the house. There was nothing more to say. What would I say to my mother? I recalled her words. One cannot change the past. All one can do is move on.

I went straight to the hospital without informing my parents. Since I was in the early stages of pregnancy, the abortion was done without much fuss. I returned home late at night. Ma was pacing up and down with worry.

"I did it. Ma. You were right. I did it," I whispered to her though I could not bring myself to look into her eyes. All the strength that I had in my body was drained. I just wanted to sleep and pretend that it was all a bad dream.

Ma understood my pain, and she helped me to bed. She tucked me in and said softly, "You made a good decision. Go to sleep and just forget everything. We will never talk about this again."

I closed my eyes and went into a deep slumber with my mother's hand on my forehead. Ma had told me to forget everything. If only it were so easy. It would forever remain as a scar in my heart. But I had to be strong. My future was waiting for me.

2
Second phase

I did eventually get over Nayan. My so-called first love was non-existent in my life. My heart was filled with terrible hatred. The guilt of aborting my child was constantly present. I didn't know whether the decision had been correct or not, but one thing I was sure of – I wouldn't have been able to handle my studies and bring up a child.

To add to it, people started talking about me. I don't know how they had got an inkling of my situation, but the word had spread. Everyone stared at me in school, and it took all my strength to not have a breakdown. My fear of my dad returned and I could never meet his eyes.

One morning, he looked at me and said, "I have found a guy for you. I have already sent them your photograph and they are ready for a meeting." He placed a photo on the TV cabinet. I didn't say a word.

I wasn't interested in meeting the guy at all. I wanted to pursue my studies but this time I knew that Papa wouldn't understand. After what had happened, I felt I could not say no.

That photograph lay untouched for a few days. The day of the visit arrived. Papa seemed very happy and had a big smile on his face. Ma was dressing me up for the meeting.

"Why didn't you tell your dad that you don't want to get married so early?" she asked.

"I don't know why, but I couldn't. I'm still guilty about what I have done."

"I told you that it was your past and you can't change it." Ma was worried about me.

"Ma, even I don't want to get married. Let me at least meet him though. It'll make Papa happy but the final decision will be mine."

"I don't know why but I don't have a good feeling about this. But it is your decision. I won't force you to do or not do anything."

She sighed and added, "There you go. You are ready. I don't think the boy will say no to you. You have to make him say no. I don't want you to leave the house so soon."

"Don't worry about that. Just trust me… everything will be fine," I mumbled. We could hear voices outside the room. They had arrived and I could hear Dad welcoming them.

"You just stay here. I'll call you after a few minutes. And please carry that tray of glasses. And be careful, you are wearing a sari."

"I'm not wearing a sari for the first time. You go and welcome them. I know how to take care of myself."

Ma went out to welcome them. I was trying to eavesdrop on the conversation. There were formal introductions taking place. And somebody from the group asked for me and Ma called out my name. With a big smile on my face, I walked out with the tray. I served each of them and my eyes finally found the prospective groom. I froze for a moment. He was very handsome and I could not take my eyes off him. Suddenly I realized that I was staring at him. I quickly went back with the tray. I told myself that I was not ready to get married.

I went out and sat facing him. I wasn't listening to anyone present and was playing with the edge of my sari. Suddenly someone said to take the guy to my room so that we could have a chat. I got up and started walking towards my room. He followed. I took a seat on my bed and he sat in front of me on a chair. There was silence for a few seconds. He broke the ice.

"My name is Sameer. And I guess yours is Maya, right?"

I just nodded my head.

Again there was a silence of a few seconds. I sighed. It was no use beating around the bush.

"Look Sameer, the truth is I don't want to get married so early. Even you're really young so why do you want to get married now?" I asked him.

"Is it too early? I don't think so. In my family, it's a tradition to get married early. By the way, I'm twenty-one if you don't know."

"That would be your thinking, Sameer, but I want to study. I want to complete my graduation. I request you to please tell your family that you don't like me."

"Why should I lie? I like you."

Neither one of us spoke for a moment. I had to put an end to this. I dared to say, "Well, I had an abortion a month back. I was having an affair with a guy."

"Hmmm… thank you for being honest. I don't mind that. I just want to know one thing – do you still love the guy?"

"That guy is as good as dead for me. He left me in a lurch. Please don't share this with either your parents or mine."

"Your secret is safe with me. But I'm glad you shared it. It doesn't really bother me at all. And I'm happy that you were honest. It would have been different if I had found out after our wedding."

I was very surprised and I admit I softened at his words. However, my studies were foremost in my mind and I couldn't compromise that even for him.

"Still Sameer, my priority is my education."

"Look, if you want to study, I will allow you to even after marriage. Even I'm in my final year and have to finish my studies. I think we both can finish our studies together. And believe me, I'm a good tutor. However, it's your decision.. I'll wait for your answer. But one thing is for sure, that I'll get married to you. And to you only."

His last sentence made me look up at him in surprise. I couldn't say a word. I wanted to say no right there and then but he didn't allow me to say a word. He got up and left.

I followed him. Everyone was staring at us with anticipation. I was tense about what Sameer would say. He went to his mother ignoring everyone and murmured something to her ears.

His mother got up from her place joined her hands and said "I think we will take our leave now."

Papa was surprised and said hurriedly, "But is it yes or no?"

"I think we need some time to decide. We'll get in touch," she said, and they left.

"You must have said something to them," Papa scolded me.

"I didn't do anything. It was their decision," I said.

"They haven't come to any decision yet. And I'll make sure that they say yes." Papa did not wait for me to reply and went inside. Ma stood staring at me.

"Tell me the truth. Why have they asked for time to decide? Hope you shared everything with him," she said.

"Ya, I shared everything with him. But he was unaffected. He said it did not matter to him. He wants to marry me and has given me time to think."

My eyes were still on the door while speaking.

"So, what are your thoughts?"

"I don't know, Ma. He doesn't mind me studying even after marriage. I'm wondering why should I say no. He's a nice guy," I revealed my feelings to Ma.

"I have one reason to reject the proposal. He is not earning yet."

"It's not a big deal, Ma. His father is quite rich, and he is about to complete his graduation. I'm sure he will get a good job in the future."

"I just want you to give it a good thought. Just don't hurry. Take your time. I have suffered a lot; I don't want you to suffer."

"Ma, I don't think I will be able to concentrate on my studies here. I need a new environment; a fresh start. I can't get Nayan or the baby out of my head. And if not him, Papa will come up with another option."

"Maya, you can't get married to someone just to get over your past. Try to get to know him first. It's a lifelong decision."

"I'm not marrying him tomorrow. We'll ask for some time."

"So I guess you have decided to get married to him."

"Ma, I'm confused but leaning towards yes."

"It's your call. I have just tried to give you a clearer perspective. If you ask me I think you should say no. I don't know why but I'm not getting good vibes."

She kissed me on my forehead and went to the kitchen. I sat down on the sofa and put on the TV. Doordarshan was the only channel back then. A television was a luxury then, and very few houses had one. My father's boss had given it to him. They said it wasn't working well, and they were planning to buy the latest model. *Byomkesh Bakshi* was an interesting new show, and I began to watch it. Soon, I fell asleep. The ringing phone woke me up.

"Ma, please pick up the phone," I said, but she didn't reply. She must have gone to her room. I got up reluctantly and picked up the phone. I said curtly, "Hello, who's that?"

"Hello, this is Sameer. I just called to inform you that we've reached home." Hearing his voice made me smile involuntarily.

"I don't care. You didn't have to call." I played a bit.

"Oh! Really? Good to know. But let me tell you that your dad told us to call him after we reach. Just tell your dad that we've reached home safely."

"I won't," I said.

"Who's called?" Papa came out of his room. I was so startled that the receiver almost dropped from my hand. I steadied myself and said, "It's for you." And I rushed to my room.

As I sat on my bed, from that short interaction I made up my mind to say yes to him. But could I tell him that? I didn't have his number. Should I ask Papa? I didn't think that would be a good idea. Suddenly I heard Papa calling me.

"Sameer wants to talk to you," he said but remained standing next to me.

"So, the call was for your dad. Good, but now it's for you. Have you thought about us?" I didn't know what to say with my dad present.

"Ya," I said a single word.

"Do share your thoughts."

"Yes." Again a single word in reply.

"I guess you are saying yes to my proposal?" he said, sounding excited.

"Ya." A smile appeared on my face and I kept the receiver down. I had said yes to him in a hurry. But was it the right decision? I felt it was. Ma was a little sceptical, but she eventually accepted my decision and showered me with lots of love.

In a few days, Sameer came back with his family bearing gifts and sweets. They had come to finalize the date of the wedding.

"The 6th of April? How would that be?" his dad said. "It is an auspicious day."

"That'll be great. We'll get enough time to spend with each other," I said.

"I think you have misunderstood. Dad is talking about next month, not next year', Sameer said.

"That would be too early, I guess. We need at least six months to prepare," said Ma.

"I think I'm okay with the date," Papa said.

"But I guess until your family is okay, we can't go ahead. Everyone should be happy," Sameer said.

"May I know the reason why you guys want it so early?" I dared to ask.

"Well, I'm planning to go abroad after my studies. I might get placed in a multinational company. After I reach there, I'll send for you," Sameer said.

"Ya, but it all depends on 'if' and 'but'. You can't decide your life on those terms," Ma reasoned.

"No, I'm not making life decisions on that at all. It's just that if I get the job overseas, I might not be able to get back to India for two or more years. And if I don't get a job overseas, I'll get a job in India. So, there won't be an issue."

Sameer seemed very clear about what he wanted in life. I kept staring at him. His handsome face was always lit up with a smile. His big eyes lent a boyish charm to his persona. So did his silky dishevelled hair.

"I'm ready," I blurted out. Everyone was happy with my decision except Ma. It was apparent on her face. Sameer got up from his place and sat in front of her.

"Aunty, trust me, nothing bad will happen. I'll take good care of her. I know you are worried about my job, but my placements are just after three months. Even my teachers believe that I'll get a good job. You might not trust me but you can trust your daughter. You know how talented she is."

He held her hand in his and promised her that he'd take care of me. Ma smiled back and relented. I, however, could still see some hesitation in her eyes. But I was happy that she had agreed.

The wedding date was around the corner. There was so much to do. Sameer used to call me twice or thrice a day, and we'd talk endlessly. Sameer's family was quite rich. His father was a wealthy businessman, and he was planning the expansion of his factory. We couldn't find any fault and Ma began coming around.

On one hand, I was busy with the wedding preparations, on the other I wanted to spend as much time as I could with Sameer. He wanted to spend all his time with me as he was quite sure that he would get admission into an overseas company. One day we went out for a movie on his Bajaj scooter. Unfortunately, the theatre was full, and the tickets sold out.

"So, what now?" I said disappointed.

"Wait, I know a place where we can go and chill."

We zoomed through the narrow streets of Ahmedabad. I had spent my entire life in Ahmedabad but it was never this beautiful. I put my head on his back as I admired the sights. Everyone was staring at us and I was enjoying the attention. I wanted to make everyone jealous. in my opinion, my to-be husband was the most handsome man in town. We rode around for a few more kilometres before stopping at Kankaria Lake.

I had been there many times with my father. But that day I had come with my fiancé. After parking his scooter, he held my hand, and we walked ahead. There were two boulders at the edge of the lake and we sat down on them. I did not want to let go of his hand. I still remember the shape of his fingers with little hair on each finger. They were warm, soft and comforting.

The wind was ruffling his hair. I glanced at his bright eyes. He was looking somewhere else. I held his chin and made him look at me. He blushed and turned his face back to the setting sun. I pulled his face towards me again. He smiled and said "What? Let me enjoy the sunset. And you should too."

"And I'm enjoying it. I couldn't find such brightness even in the rising sun. Your hands are warmer than the rays of the rising sun. The lake is lucky that you are sitting here. You have added a feather to its beauty. Thank you for bringing me here," I said and leaned my head on his shoulder.

"If I'm a feather, then you are the bird. I don't have any value without you. I have no meaning if I'm not with you. I'll make you fly as high as you can."

He put his finger under my chin and made me look at him. We stared at each other and soon were sharing a passionate kiss. My eyes filled with tears.

"Hey what happened to you?" he asked.

"Thank you for accepting me the way I am. You knew my past and still want me to be yours. I'm so lucky to have you in my life."

"You know when you shared the truth with me, I was rather shocked. But the fact that you trusted me to share your secret, helped me to make up my mind."

"So, you love me the most, right?"

"No, my first love is my dad. You come second. I respect him a lot and I just don't have words for his goodness."

"And you might be my third. First is my mother, second is the guy I told you about and then you."

"You are going to get punished for this..." He threw some water from the lake on me and ran away. I ran behind him to take revenge. We came to a stop, panting. Sameer came close and held my hands.

"Thank you for accepting me."

That was the happiest moment of my life.

Why didn't my life just stop there? Couldn't I just have pressed 'pause' at that very moment? However, you have to go with the flow. At that moment, Sameer was everything to me. I just wanted to follow in his footsteps, not knowing that they were leading me towards the darkness.

3

Third phase

Sameer was the one who gave me a second life by accepting my past. It wasn't an easy thing to do. Most of my relatives would taunt me but Ma always told me to ignore them and not pay any heed to their unkind words. Sameer's foray into my life was a slap on their faces and they retreated sheepishly.

After our wedding, I postponed taking admission to a college for my graduation. Sameer told me I could do so the following year after I settled down. He, meanwhile, began to prepare for his placement interviews. He was determined to get into a company overseas. And I had absolutely no doubt that he would. Not only Sameer, but his family accepted me with a big heart as well. Being a single child, I loved to spend time with each family member.

It was our one-month marriage anniversary. Everyone was quite happy, and we had planned a small party for that day. My parents had come earlier that day to help with the preparations. New love and new marriage always bring much excitement in life. You often get bewildered. Ma's presence was such a relief for me. I was still in the process of getting used to living with his family. They weren't bad at all but accepting this house as mine was quite difficult for me. It was a new house, with new rules, and I couldn't be a queen as I had been at my parents' house.

The party was a big hit. It was perfect in every way. We made a handsome couple and everyone's eyes were on us. Sameer introduced me to his guests, and I mingled with everyone at ease.

By the end of the party, I had as many friends as Sameer did. It went on well into the night. We were dog-tired when it was finally over and wanted to hit the sack.

"Sameer, please can you bring some water from downstairs?" I insisted.

"I'm not going. I don't have any energy left," he said, yawning.

"Please, Sameer."

I went near and kissed him. He responded with a kiss but I interrupted him midway.

"First water, please. My throat is parched. And something else is drenched. I'll wait for you," I teased him.

"Okay," he said with a grin and went down.

As I was waiting for him to return, I heard him let out a scream. I ran downstairs. I saw Sameer sitting on the floor. His father was lying unconscious on the floor and Sameer was trying to revive him.

"Dad, please wake up, Dad! What happened to you?" Sameer seemed terrified and was crying uncontrollably.

"Sameer, we should take him to the hospital," I cried and called for an ambulance. He was lying on the floor and as I checked, he wasn't breathing at all. We rushed him to the hospital, but the doctors declared him dead. He had suffered a heart attack and could not be revived.

It was a terrible blow for Sameer who had been so close to him. He was shattered. I tried to support him but he chose to deal with his grief alone. We finished all the rituals in a few days. A demise just after a month of our wedding was quite disturbing for me. I was shaken but Sameer was unable to deal with such a huge loss; after all, he had worshipped his father. Even after a month, he was not himself.

Meanwhile, my body began to feel different. They were the same symptoms I had experienced during my first pregnancy. I was sure that I was pregnant. I was crestfallen as I did not want a child so early. I wanted to resume my studies. I couldn't talk to Sameer at that time so I went to his mother.

"Mom, may I?" I asked before entering the room.

"You should be with Sameer. He needs you. A woman can handle any pain but for a man, it is quite difficult."

"Mom, I need to tell you something. As of now I only can share this with you."

"If you feel it's more important than Sameer, then go ahead."

"I don't know whether it's more important or not, but I have taken a decision that might affect him."

She just looked at me questioningly.

"Mom, I'm pregnant but I don't want this child," I said clearly.

"That's good news, beta. That will certainly help Sameer recover. But wait, what did you just say? You don't want the child? Did I hear you correctly?"

"Mom, you heard it right. I want to pursue my studies. Sameer is not in a state to talk. Please, Mom, help me. What should I do?"

"Do not kill your child. That might end up killing Sameer as well. He won't be able to handle two shocks at a time. I know him. The final decision will be yours. It's just that I don't want two widows in one house."

I decided to talk to Sameer about it but I was afraid. I decided to give him the news of my pregnancy first. I wanted to see his reaction. Then I would take the second step accordingly.

"I wanted to tell you something. I guess I'm pregnant, Sameer," I murmured as we got ready to sleep.

He remained silent for a few seconds and rolled back to me with tears in his eyes. He hugged me and said, "Thank you for giving me such wonderful news after such a long time. I needed this. I can be happy again. I know my dad is coming back to this world."

I didn't know how to react. He didn't even ask me what I wanted. I guess it was more important to make him feel better at that point in time. So, I decided to discuss the part later.

As time passed, Sameer came out of his grief. My pregnancy helped him to return to his normal self. I could see the happiness on his face. I allowed him to be happy. It was time to share my problem with him. So, one day, I made his favourite dishes and decided to talk to him when he got back from college. It was the day of his campus selection and I was sure that he'd get selected. Once that was settled, I could broach the topic of abortion.

I was eagerly waiting for him to return home. I bought some sweets from a nearby shop and wore some new clothes as well. It was going to be a special evening, and I was waiting to celebrate his success. The sun was about to set, and the golden sky reminded me of the day by the lake. I smiled at the memory.

After a few minutes, I heard Sameer walk in. I ran to him but was surprised to see the state he was in. His face was red and so were his eyes. He was reeking of alcohol.

"What's wrong Sameer?" I asked as I steadied him.

"I didn't get the bloody placement. Anything else you want to know?" he snarled at me and pushed me aside.

"It's not a big deal, Sameer. You can still get a good job in another company. "

This was unexpected and not a part of the plan. I tried to console him but it was wiser to remain silent because of the state he was in.

"I wanted a job in an overseas company. There were ten overseas companies that had come to our college. I couldn't crack even a single one. There must be something wrong with me. That's why I couldn't get the job."

He began to get furious. I made him put his head on my shoulder and allowed him to vent. I held his face and brought it in front of me. His face was drenched with tears. I wiped away his tears and said, "Look at me."

He rolled up his eyes and looked into mine.

"You can't be so weak. You have to take care of three lives now. Mom has got the job of a chef at a restaurant. We have some savings as well and we have time. I trust you and I know you would do anything for our baby."

I took his hand and kept it on my belly. He blew his nose and hugged me back and said, "Thank you for your support. I know I'll get a good job in an overseas company. I won't accept failure so easily. I'll try for our son."

"It could be a daughter too," I said and then resolved to have the baby. If making him happy brought me so much happiness, why not have a baby? I would go through with the pregnancy solely for him. However, his desire for a son was causing me some concern.

"I know Dad is coming back. So don't be worried we'll be blessed with a baby boy."

I didn't argue. Sameer was getting back to normal, and that is what mattered the most. He promised me that he wouldn't overthink and would move ahead. He applied to many other companies, but luck seemed to evade him. After months of trying, he gave up. He lost his focus and determination after all the rejections he faced. He had made some friends in the meantime and began to loaf around with them.

His behaviour began to change, and we started fighting very often. We were running out of money. Mom and I decided to sell the house and move into a smaller one. We bought a small house and put the rest of the money in the bank. I hoped that after the baby would come, he'd pay heed to his responsibilities.

In a few months, the baby was born. It was a baby girl. I was going through mixed emotions. I was elated to have my daughter beside me but was worried about how Sameer would react. He had fervently hoped for a boy after all. After a while, the doctor sent him into the room. A smile on his face brought some relief to me. He came close and sat on a stool next to the bed.

"Look at her. She's so beautiful. That's my angel."

The happiness of becoming a father was clearly visible on his face. He started making cooing sounds to get her attention. I stared at his handsome face and held his hand.

"She's just like you. I love you, Sameer. Thank you for accepting her and showering her with love."

"I should say thank you for giving me such a beautiful daughter. Dad might have delayed his trip back, but he has sent an angel to us," he said with tears in his eyes.

I wiped his tears, kissed him on his forehead, and then kissed my daughter's head. We held each other tightly. People say that a daughter brings good luck, so I hoped that things would turn for us. And it did to some extent.

Sameer found a job. It wasn't a high-paying one, but he said he would work anywhere for his child. I started helping Mom make food for the restaurant as well as for some hostellers nearby. With the three of us working, life seemed to be getting better.

Mom was gaining weight day by day. In a year she put on a hundred kilos. It was becoming difficult for her to go out and work but she continued. Our daughter turned one and a half, so now her requirements were increasing as well. I accidentally became pregnant again. Our dream to have a boy child literally convinced me to continue with the pregnancy. Sameer started working but could not stick to one company for long. He used to change his job often. We carried on nevertheless.

After nine months, a second baby girl was born to us. I was worried but Sameer didn't seem to mind, though he wasn't as pleased as the first time. His mother wasn't happy at all but what could she do? I looked at the tiny angelic face of my little baby girl. My heart was filled with love and I vowed to cherish and take care of her no matter what the circumstances.

I was just twenty-one and now had two children to take care of. I had forgotten all about resuming my studies. It didn't seem possible. Taking care of two children and Mom was quite difficult as it is. Sameer, in the meantime, had lost his job yet again. I still had two or three hostellers whom I was feeding, but I slowly began to lose them one at a time, when I couldn't manage to take out enough time to cook. Sameer and his mom weren't happy with the two girls, so they forced me to have another pregnancy. The third turned out to be another girl and so did the fourth.

At the age of twenty-eight, I had four daughters. I looked at myself in the mirror. What had I done to myself? I was fighting endlessly for food and money. We literally ran out of money during those years. I was blamed for all the bad luck. Having a girl child was my fault and the loss of their father after we got married was my fault too. We finished every penny that they had saved. That was my fault. So was the failure of the tiffin business. Why was it always me? I had aged and looked like I was in my forties.

I decided to take matters into my own hands. I would go out to work and feed the family. I tidied myself up. I combed my hair, fixed my saree neatly, washed my face, and put on some makeup. I smile at my reflection in the mirror, wiping away the tears from the corners of my eyes.

"Mom, I think I should look for a job," I said approaching her.

"Job? What is this new idea? Forget it. Concentrate on the few students we have left. Otherwise, we will lose them as well." She was furious.

"Mom, I'm not asking you. I'm telling you. I have always listened to you. Now let me listen to myself," I said as I went back to my room.

She kept grumbling as I locked the door. I didn't have a degree so I couldn't hope for a job that needed a graduate degree. But I hoped to get one on the basis of my looks. I had to make myself presentable. I chose a plain dark yellow saree. Thankfully even after delivering four babies, my belly was flat, and I draped the saree carefully.

I put on my makeup to hide the spots of neglect over the years. I tried different hairstyles, but in the end decided to leave my hair open. I looked nice but something was still missing. I looked around and found a pink scarf with yellow flowers printed on it. I used it as a hairband and that completed my look.

I loved the person I saw in the mirror. I was reminded of my former self. Mom brought me back to reality. "Open the bloody door, your kids are crying!" she shouted.

I opened the door. She stared at me in surprise. I picked up my little one, kissed her and handed her over to Mom.

"She's not only my responsibility. She's your son's responsibility too."

"Don't you dare to go out without my permission. Think about your kids at least. They won't be able to survive without their mother," she warned me.

"And don't you dare to stop me now! Otherwise, I won't ever come back. I'm going out only for their survival," I replied.

She could not fight anymore. She glared at me for a few seconds but I didn't care. I walked out with determination.

I had to look for a job that didn't require much educational qualification. And the first thing that came to my mind was working as a salesgirl. I decided to try my luck at a cosmetic shop.

I went into a shop. A middle-aged man was sitting inside.

"Sir, is there any vacancy for me?"

He just shook his head. I tried to explain my desperation to him but he didn't even look up. I tried a few more cosmetic stores in vain. I was tired and sat down on a bench. I wiped my sweaty brow and took out some water to drink. Suddenly my eyes went to an advertisement board '*Nokari mate malo*' (*Meet for job*). It was a men's accessories showroom. There was no harm in giving it a try. I freshened up and went to look for the shop.

I entered the shop. It had a glass door with a long stainless steel handle. I looked in but couldn't find anyone inside. I decided to wait for a while for someone to appear.

I began observing the things in the shop. It was a small shop, but the owner had arranged the wares neatly. It was hardly a ten by twenty feet showroom. There were belts, wallets, chains, jeans and so on. The shop had everything that a man needed. There were some cassettes in a corner along with small hand video games which I could never afford for my kids. I also found an opened video game console with some repair tools lying on the table. I guessed the shop also carried out repairs.

I stepped ahead to find something strange lying under the table. It was locked with a glass cover and had a sticker pasted on it.

"Hey you, what do you want?"

A person of my age entered the shop. He was wearing a blue-coloured shirt which was quite loose. He had tucked his shirt in such a way that it created a round tiny balloon around his west. His belt was half visible. He was wearing bell-bottom pants. His hair was rather long. They covered both his ears. He was wearing extra-large goggles which he took off while talking to me. He certainly was a fashionista.

"I saw a board outside. I think you guys have a vacancy. And I'm in need of a job," I said.

"Ya, but that job is for a man. We don't require a woman."

"Sir, your products are for men but there are better chances of them being sold if the salesperson is a woman."

He looked at me and then went to the counter. He turned to me and observed me for a few seconds and said "But I guess this outfit won't work. And would you be able to sell the products?"

"No sir, I won't sell the products. That part will be taken care of by you. I'll just make them realize that they need your products in their life. I'll make the product necessary for them. I guess that would work for you."

"We'll discuss the salary after you make me believe that you can sell the products," he said.

I wanted to jump as high as I could but I controlled myself. I put a smile on my face and told him I'd join the next day. It was a great achievement for me. I tried not to cry but didn't succeed. I wiped off my tears and went back home with a happy heart.

The very next day, I started working, and the owner was quite happy with me. The sales increased, and I loved the job. The boss was good to me too. He took care of the men's innerwear section. The owner was of my age but I never received any unwanted attention from him. Not only him, but his family was good as well. His wife was concerned about me and always enquired about my girls. The owner considered me as his sister and forced me to tie a rakhi on his hand.

The problem was my family members. Sameer and Mom could not bear to see that I was earning more than Sameer. Sameer said that he was earning well, but after I started working, he never gave me any money to run the house. In fact, I was afraid that he was lying and didn't have a job at all. And my doubt solidified when I saw him sitting idly with his friends. How could he be so irresponsible? He was not the same guy I had met earlier. My mom was right. I shouldn't have agreed to get married so early. He seemed pristine from the outside, but I didn't know when he turned black from inside.

We started fighting every single day. And like always, Mom took his side. People used to say that I didn't care about my daughters, but I knew that I was working only for them. They'd cry every morning as I would leave the house, but I knew that it was better to cry at that moment than in the future. I wanted to educate them so that they'd never have to be dependent on anyone.

I started spending more time at my workplace. I kind of started ignoring people around me, especially my husband and Mom. I focused on my job. A month passed by and I was fed up with my family. My boss and rakhi brother, Madhav knew what was going on.

"Why don't you divorce him?" Madhav said.

"It's not that easy, Madhav. I have to take care of my daughters. And you know divorce is not a small word in my community.

They had issues when I started working, how will they ever accept a divorce?"

"Do you really care about them? I guess you are bold. You can do anything you want. You don't need a man to support you," he said.

"Thank you for believing me, but I don't think it's the right time. I want to give him a chance. It has only been a month. He might learn something, seeing me working so hard."

Before I could say anything more, a person entered the shop. He had black sunglasses on and was dressed in a garish manner. His hair was dishevelled and gold chains hung from his neck. The top buttons of his shirt were open. He seemed like a typical 'gunda'.

"I want these songs to be recorded. I'll come tomorrow and will collect them." He handed me a paper on which the names of a few songs were written. He did not look at me and left. I read the names and coincidentally they were my favourite as well. But it was quite impossible to collect those songs from the internet. Searching for them and downloading them would be hectic work.

"Wait, we might take some time, so you better come the day after tomorrow," I said.

He stopped there and glared at me. He came close, locking eyes with me. "If you are saying that, then I'm ready to wait."

"Hey Kabir, just stay away, she's my sister!" Madhav said.

"As far as I know you don't have any sisters, or if you do, your parents are too fast," he smirked.

"Mind your language, Mr Whatever, he's like my brother and his family is mine. So why don't you just get out and carry on," I yelled at him.

He looked at me again, smiled and said "So sorry, ma'am. Take your time. I'll be back after two days,"

He did not wait for my reply and went out. I was furious.

"Bhai, why do you allow such people to enter the shop?" I asked.

"We have to entertain every kind of customer. It's just that we have to be careful. And you don't know this guy; it's better to stay away from such people. So, let's just do our work. I don't know why he didn't shout back at you, but just stay away from him," Madhav said in a serious tone.

"Maybe because he was scolded by a lady for the first time," I laughed.

I looked at his song list and decided to do the work the following day. I finished all my other work on that day and went home early. I was being paid a good amount. But as I was the only earning member in the house, feeding seven people at home and meeting the requirements of each one was not possible and I'd always fall short. Somehow I managed by compromising my own needs. After making their bed, I sat down to tell my three girls a story. The youngest was already fast asleep.

I told them the story of Sati, and how she brought her husband back from Yamraj. My eldest daughter was still awake, while the other three had fallen asleep. She kept her hand on my chin and made me look at her.

"Mom, if Dad dies, will you go to Yama?"

"As a human, I can go to save any living creature."

"Mom, you are so good, then why is Dad always fighting with you? I have seen a movie in which the heroine gets a divorce from the hero. No, actually he wasn't a hero, he was a bad guy like Dada. Then they were living in different places and the heroine got a new dada for her daughter. Why can't you give divorce to Dada?" she asked innocently.

I understood that she had been noticing our fights. That scared me. I put her to sleep without answering her question. I couldn't sleep that whole night though as I was in another state of mind.

In the morning, I left home after making their meals. I reached the shop. Madhav had some work, so he was not coming in. I would be alone. I began with the recording work first. The moron's work. He might be a moron, but I admit I admired his taste in music. I started humming each song while copying them to the cassette.

"Mubarake tumhe ke tum... kisi ke noor ho gaye...

Kisi ke itne paas ho... ke sabse dur ho gaye..."

I heard a voice behind me sing.

It was the same fellow. He entered the shop again and continued singing, *"Ajib dastaan hai yeh... kahan shuru kahan khatam..."*

"Your recording is not done yet. I told you that I would take two days. So please come tomorrow."

"I need some other things," he replied.

"Okay, what do you want?" I sighed.

"I want a leather belt, very smooth and black," he said grinning.

Without saying a word, I picked up a bunch of belts, tossed them in front of him and said with a fake smile on my face, "Have a look and select one. Then pay and get lost."

"Okay, you don't have to get so agitated. Anyway, thank you."

He started looking at the belts. He'd steal glances at me while humming,

"Kisi ka pyar leke tum naya jahan basaoge..."

I was fuming, but I didn't react. In a few minutes, four boys came in. One of them came to me and asked about Madhav.

"He's not coming today. May I help you, sir?" I said.

"I want underwear. Will you help me with that?"

They all laughed, but those cheap lines didn't affect me. I took out the boxes and started showing him one after another. My hands were trembling, and I started sweating. Observing me, one of them commented *"Itne me hi pasina nikal gaya?"*

And the rest started laughing again.

"I mean to say show us more," he grinned and came closer.

"Hi guys, my name is Kabir. I guess I won't mind showing you the things."

Kabir came over to me. He took over and started showing them the products. I had a good look at him. He had applied mascara in his eyes. He was wearing a bracelet in one hand. A tight t-shirt was showing his muscles. He wasn't looking at the products he was presenting but was staring into the eyes of the boys. The fear was clearly visible on their faces. They soon bolted out of the door like cowards without buying anything.

"Thank you, Kabir, it means a lot. I'm glad that you were there."

"By the way, which underwear will suit me?"

He picked up one and kept it on his pants and started laughing. I threw one at his face.

"You are a moron too. But thank you."

"Don't be worried. I'm writing down my number on this paper. Just feel free to call. I won't ask for your number. This number is only for an emergency."

He left, and I remained staring at him. I developed a soft spot for him. Why wasn't my own husband so caring? I suppose there was no point in even thinking about him.

Those chaps returned frequently to tease me. I used to make a call to Kabir's landline. Within a few minutes of my call, he used to reach the shop and would drive the boys away. I wasn't aware when these emergency calls got converted to friendly calls. I kept it hidden from Madhav. Everything happened when Madhav was not in the shop.

During that period our fights at home were terrible. Kabir didn't care about what people would think. He'd come home bearing gifts for everyone, especially Mom. Mom looked forward to his visits, and so did the girls. His visits became very frequent.

One night, when I was putting the girls to bed, the eldest told me, "Mom, why don't you get married to Kabir uncle? He's a nice guy. He also takes care of us," she said.

"From where do these silly thoughts come into your mind? You know that I'm married and your dad is still alive. And why am I even discussing this with you? Don't dream impossible dreams," I whispered.

That night I stopped her. But it was difficult to stop the people surrounding us. And as I was afraid, the news reached Madhav as well. He warned me to stay away from him. But there was nothing between us. We were just good friends. So I didn't care about what people were saying. I shared my thoughts with Madhav too. He came around but I could sense that he disliked Kabir for some reason.

"Madhav, I'm tensed and I think I should leave him." I shared my thoughts with Madhav.

"I've been telling you for ages that he's not good for you. You should leave him."

"Ya, but I'm worried about my daughters. How will I take care of them after the divorce?" I said.

"What the hell! You were talking about Sameer? I thought you were talking about Kabir. So, I was right… there's something between you and Kabir."

"Not at all, Madhav. It's just that I want to get separated from Sameer. Kabir has nothing to do with that. I'm just worried about my kids."

"If it is so then you don't need to be worried about them. I'll take care of them. I don't have any children and as the doctors have said I won't be having any in the future. I would like to raise them as mine."

"Oh thank you. Are you sure? I thought you wouldn't support me."

I couldn't look at him. I kept looking upwards.

"If you hadn't told me, I would have told you to do so. I'm glad that you've taken such a bold decision. But your journey won't be easy after that."

"If you are with me, I don't need to be worried, bhai. I know my daughters are always safe with you," I replied gratefully.

It wasn't easy for a woman like me to fight against the community, especially in that era when we weren't even allowed to go out without covering our faces. I was glad that I could get a job and earn for my family. And all thanks to Madhav who supported me. Without him, nothing would have been possible. He was more to me than my real parents. Everything looked better after I met him. I sent a divorce notice to my husband. He didn't get furious as I had expected he would. Instead, he started crying.

"I'm sorry that I could not make you happy. You can go and live your life happily. Just one request, please don't take our daughters with you," he begged me.

But, how was I supposed to leave the children with him? He was not even earning. And his mom was not in a condition to take care of all of them. She was taking care of them the whole day but in the evening they needed me.

"Please Sameer, you at least have your mom. I don't have anyone with me. I don't know about them, but I need them. A mom needs her children. Please let me have them. I have asked you for many things but you never gave me anything. This is the last time I'm asking for something which you can give without an argument," I bent down on a knee and pleaded with him. I let my tears flow.

"Okay, okay… just listen to me."

He held me from my shoulders and helped me up.

"I have a solution. Why don't you take two of them with you? I'll take care of the other two. I promise I will work for them and I'll do anything to feed them. Please trust me, Maya."

I looked into his eyes. He was in a lot of pain. But that didn't mean I would let go of my daughters. And why would I trust him?

"They are not properties, Sameer. We can't divide them. They are born to be with each other."

"We were made to be with each other. Now we are separating. And somebody has to pay for that, Maya," he said, holding my hands.

"We should pay for that, not our kids, Sameer. I know we both love them but somebody has to compromise. And I can't trust a guy who is not earning."

I wiped off my tears and said firmly, "My decision is final. My daughters will always remain with me, no matter what."

I didn't wait for his answer. I took my luggage and my daughters with me. Yes, there had been bad experiences in that house but I loved Sameer a lot. My earlier days were beautiful, and I cherished those memories. I was attached to the house and now I was leaving. But leaving those things behind was essential for me. I could see a brighter future. Something new was waiting outside. I left my house with a lot of hope, leaving the bad memories behind.

I thought that would be the last time that I would cry. But you don't know what destiny has decided for you. I shifted in with Madhav and his family. Though it wasn't easy for me and my daughters to accept the change, Madhav and his family made us feel at home. They took care of us. Madhav had handed over the shop to me. I began to look after the purchases and sales of the shop. Madhav was making his foray into politics. His in-laws came from a powerful political family, and according to them, Madhav was quite a good candidate for their party.

"Bhaiya, you have given me all the responsibility. I had to hire two more people under me. I don't know whether everything is going well or not. Please bhaiya, I need you here," I said when he had come to the shop one day.

"I trust you, and you are earning way more than I was. So, you are definitely doing well. But I have heard about something else too. And I have come here to discuss that with you." He looked a bit worried.

"Ask me anything."

"Let me come to the point. Kabir. I don't like his frequent visits. He is not a good guy."

"Madhav bhaiya, you know that we are just good friends and nothing else. You don't need to be worried about that. And I don't know why you have that perception of him. He may look scruffy but he is a good person," I explained.

"I know him better than you do. Please do as I say."

"You know me as well, Madhav. Trust me, I have no feelings like that."

"I'm letting him go because I trust you, but I'll be keeping a close watch."

This avatar of Madhav – a loving and caring brother – was new to me. I had to obey him. So, I decided to stay away from Kabir for a while but Kabir would have none of it. He tried to meet up for a few days but failed. He knew I was avoiding him. Finally one morning he arrived at the shop.

"Hey Maya, how are you?"

"I'm all good. Do you want anything?"

"Ya, but I wonder if you will be able to give it."

"What do you mean?"

"I want to spend the rest of my life with you. Will you marry me?" he asked straight away. I was very surprised. This was completely unexpected.

"Kabir, I don't feel anything for you and this is quite shocking for me. Kabir, you are my good friend. I've been keeping my distance because Madhav does not like us to be close. Please try to understand, Kabir. I'm okay with your friendship but not marriage. I'll deal with Madhav, but let's just be friends and nothing more please."

"You know what, Maya? I like the way you handle things. Fine, let's just be friends."

4

Hide and Seek

"Maya, I'm not talking to you," Madhav said to me on the phone.

"Now what's the problem?"

"I told you to stay away from Kabir. I've got to know from my sources that you are still meeting him."

"Madhav, as I said earlier, we are just good friends. He comes to the shop, I just can't throw him out, can I? Madhav, don't be worried about me, please focus on your elections. In the next six months, your party's future is going to be decided."

"You focus on the shop and don't worry about the party. I'm a bit worried about you, sis. Anyway, there's good news. The party was happy with my work. They have handed me the leadership, and if our party wins I might be the next CM."

"Oh Madhav, that's great news. I know you'll be the CM. You deserve that. Best of luck," I said and kept the receiver down.

"Guess what, I got the pager. Now you can call me at any time and I'll receive a text message in this small gadget," Kabir was waiting for me to end the call.

"Pager? Now what the hell is that? Let me see."

He gave me the gadget. A small square gadget, black in colour, had a very small screen. Kabir showed me some short messages he had got.

"Quite nice. I don't think I need to worry now," I said.

"Ya, I'm always there for you. Just a message away now," he said, trying to come close to me. However, I stepped back looking for a stool.

"Kabir, can you please check there? I can't find the stool."

"Why do you need the stool?"

"I just want to put this radio on the top shelf. This one's the least in demand."

"I guess you don't need the stool then."

Kabir came behind the counter and knelt down.

"You can use my leg as a stool. Just be careful... you are quite heavy," he said with a grin.

I didn't answer and kept my leg on his. I tried to hoist myself up but he could not take my weight. He lost his balance and I found myself in his lap. I tried to get up but fell over him. Our faces were very close and our eyes met. He tucked my hair behind my ears and before I knew it, his soft lips touched mine. I could not resist and kissed him back. Was it wrong? I could not decide that but at that moment I wanted him. I wanted to kiss him again. He stopped for a moment and stood up.

"No, I promised you nothing more than a friendship," he said.

"Ya, you are absolutely right. But I guess it was just an accident, right?"

"Ya absolutely right," he said but came back and kissed me.

"Stop... stop..." I said and pushed him back. "We need to control ourselves, Kabir."

He went out without saying anything. I felt like I had done something wrong. I was so sure that there was nothing between us then why did that happen? I should have controlled myself. I decided to stay away from him. However, it was he who started ignoring me. There were no calls and he stopped dropping in at the shop. I was worried about him. I know he was doing that to avoid any such accidents again. Then why the hell was I so worried about him? I focused on my shop and waited for two more days. But there was no sign of him.

I could not bear it any longer so I finally decided to call him. I called his landline number and after ringing for quite a while, somebody picked up the phone.

"Hello, who's this?" a strange voice said.

"Kabir?"

"Sir is not well. He can't take the call."

The words scared me.

"What do you mean by that? What has happened to him?"

"He met with an accident four days back."

I dropped the phone and hurriedly closed the shop. I hailed an auto and went straight to his house. Without ringing the doorbell I pushed to open the main door and entered the house. I found Kabir sitting on a sofa and watching television.

I was furious. I was panicking and there he was laughing and watching TV. I went near him and snatched the remote from his hands.

"What the hell is this, Kabir? Somebody said that you met with an accident a few days back. And you are watching this bloody big box!"

"Ya, that's true. I fell from a chair. Not a big thing, I guess. And that was an accident."

Kabir was making me more furious.

"I don't think I should even talk to you," I turned around and started walking out. He held my hand and pulled me back. We came close to each other. His one hand went up my back and with the other, he was holding my other hand. The wind of the fan was ruffling our hair. Our eyes met. I tried to move away but Kabir was holding me so tightly that I could not move or didn't try hard enough to.

"You came here because you care for me. It affects you if I'm not well. I did this just to make you realize that you care and you love me too," he whispered.

Maybe he was right. I was still trying to free myself from his arms with a little force.

"Not for the third time, Kabir. I'm scared. I'm scared of love. I don't think there's anything like love in my life," I said with a broken voice still in his arms and struggling to get free.

"Believe me this time you won't regret it. Let yourself free, Maya. Don't just bind yourself. Be a free bird. Do what you like. Express yourself. Let the love come out of you. I know everything about your past. Just forget your past and marry me. I can't live without you."

I could feel his arms around me. His eyes could not lie and that reminded me of our last kiss. I kissed him without thinking of the repercussions. That seemed to be the yes to his question. I was a bit scared because this was the third time that I was falling in love. I did not know whether it was love or just an attraction, but I considered it as love.

The big thing was to convince Madhav. I knew that he wouldn't be happy with this relationship. I tried to convince Kabir to take it slow, but he wanted to get married as fast as possible.

"Look Maya, I can't stay without you even for a single day. Let's just get married," he said.

"Kabir, I have to talk to Madhav. And he is out of town for a few days. Let him come then we'll decide," I said.

"What if he says no?"

"He won't say no. I know him very well. I know how to convince him."

"And I know him too. I know he will never accept me. Maya, let's just get married before he arrives."

"Kabir, it's just a matter of a few days. And trust me I know how to convince Madhav."

"I trust you. I know you can convince him even after our marriage. We are not breaking our relationship with him. Wait, is it the trust issue? You don't trust me, right?"

"It's nothing like that, Kabir. I do trust you. I just need to inform him. He's my brother, Kabir."

"He's not your real brother, Maya. And I guess you are just making excuses. I don't believe you. I think you don't want to get married."

After listening to his words, I sighed and took a deep breath.

"Okay, let's just get married. I'll convince Madhav. But till then you won't say anything to anyone. This marriage will be a secret. Once Madhav is convinced, we'll tell him the truth."

"Thank you, Maya. I was so scared. You've made me feel better now," he hugged me and said.

We decided to have a registered marriage. I could not stop myself from sharing the news with Madhav's wife Meera. Meera supported me and promised that she wouldn't share anything with Madhav until he got back. She signed as a witness in the registrar's office. Kabir got two more friends with him, and we got married in the presence of three witnesses.

My life was going to start again. Something struck my mind on the first night of our marriage and I decided to speak to Kabir about it. I knew it was late but it was essential to talk to him. I was waiting for Kabir to enter the room. He came with a few papers in his hands.

"What's that?" I asked him.

"Tickets to Mumbai. We are leaving tomorrow."

"Madhav is returning tomorrow evening. We have to talk to him before we leave."

"Maya, you can meet him when we get back. We are going only for two days. And I guess your brother is in town for a week."

"But I want to tell him the truth. I don't want him to hear it from anyone else. He will be hurt."

"Look Maya," he said as he caught my chin and made me look at him. "Now we are married. Nothing will change and frankly, I don't care about Madhav's reaction. The thing is you are all mine now. No one can take you away from me. So, please say yes. I have booked our room in a five-star hotel. So, I just want you to wait till tomorrow. I'm not going to do anything today," he said and smiled at me.

"Kabir, I would like to share something else too. But I'm afraid."

"Are you mad? Why are you afraid of me? Please feel free, Maya. This is your house now."

"Kabir, I don't want to have children. And you know I already have four daughters. I want two of them to live with us, if you don't mind," I asked hesitantly.

He took a deep breath and said, "Look Maya, why do you want only two of them? All four of them are adorable. They are my kids too. Just get them all here."

I looked at him and felt relieved.

"Thank you, Kabir. I knew my decision to get married to you

was right. Even I want all of them back in my life. But I'm afraid that Sameer won't agree. I could ask for two at least."

Kabir went back to get a glass of water and said, "That will be your decision, Maya, I can't interfere in your past. So just do what you want. Just make it clear that I'm okay with whatever you decide. I just want to spend the rest of my life with you… nothing else."

He came close to me and kissed me. I removed his kurta and kissed him back. His body was in good shape and his chest was smooth. Suddenly he stopped in between and said, "I want to save my energy for tomorrow."

"Never mind," I said and leaned back on my bed. He took his place beside me and we both went to sleep. The next morning he woke up early and commenced packing. It seemed like he was in a big hurry.

"We have a lot of time to pack, right?"

"Ya, but I'm quite excited. I haven't done anything. And I can't wait to reach the hotel. And it'll be great if we reach the airport early," he said.

"But I'll take time."

"No, you won't because I have packed your things as well. Just freshen up and we are ready to go,"

"What? Well, thank you."

I got up from the bed and went to hug him. Suddenly the door burst open and Madhav entered the house. He went and hit Kabir. I ran towards him to stop him but he pushed me aside.

"I told you to stay away from him! Thank god I got here on time. This crook was planning to sell you in Mumbai."

I didn't want to believe him. His words broke me. Surely, it couldn't be true!

"He's my husband, Madhav. How can you say something like that?" I said with fear on my face.

"Just wait," he said and started searching for something. Kabir was still lying on the floor, moaning in pain. I ignored him and waited for Madhav's answer. He went near Kabir and checked his pocket and found his pager. He took it out and kicked him one more time. Kabir screamed in pain again.

"This pager will give us the proof. And let me check his landline."

He picked up the receiver, pressed the redial button on the instrument and kept it on speaker.

> "*Hello Bhai, Kabir bol rela hu. Nikal rela hu ab (Hello, this is Kabir. I'm leaving in a while).*" Madhav pretended to be Kabir.
>
> "*Tere ko bole la hain nikal te time pe phone mat kiya kar. Ab kisi aur ko phone nikalne ke baad karna. Aur sun ladki theek hain na? Varna party se pura paisa nai milega. (I have told you not to call when you are leaving. Don't call again after you leave. And listen, is the girl okay? Otherwise, the party won't pay the full amount for her.)*"
>
> "*Ekdam kadak hain boss. Chalo main rakhta hu varna woh sun legi. (She is perfectly fine. I'm hanging up now; else, she will hear us.)*"

Madhav put down the receiver and ended the call. I still couldn't believe that it was true.

"Why didn't you inform me earlier?" I said after reality had sunk in.

"Maya, you promised me that you wouldn't meet Kabir anymore. And you told me to trust you. So I did. You should have at least told me that you were getting married to him. But anyway, thanks to my sources I reached here on time. Else this man would have sold you in an Arab country. You want to see what is in your bag?" Without waiting for my answer he opened the bag and showed me the burkha.

"This was his plan. After reaching Mumbai he would inject you with some steroid and make you unconscious and cover you with this burkha."

I was numb with shock. Before we could finish our talk, a bullet went through Madhav's chest with a loud bang. I covered my ears with my hands and screamed. Suddenly I felt a sharp pain at the back of my head and I crumpled to the floor. I opened my eyes and saw Madhav on the floor, bleeding. I could see the blurred face of Kabir as he went near Madhav and kicked him. I raised my hand to stop him but I was too weak. Before I knew it, I lost consciousness.

5

The Struggle

Was I dreaming? I saw Kabir, Madhav and myself in one room. Madhav was explaining why I was wrong when suddenly Kabir woke up and started searching for something. Another version of me was standing in the corner observing the scene. I seemed to be a spirit. Finally, Kabir found the gun that he had hidden below his bed. He pointed the gun at Madhav while I was still arguing with him. The spirit me ran towards Kabir and tried to stop him but couldn't touch him. It was like she was invisible. A bullet burst out of the gun and hit Madhav's chest.

I screamed his name, "Madhav!"

My eyes opened with a start. I found myself in a dark place. My hands and legs were tied and my mouth was taped. It seemed like I was in the boot of a car. I was scared and started sweating. I tried to get my hands and legs free but in vain. So, I began to strike my head on the body of the car, hoping someone would hear me. Suddenly the car screeched to a halt. I heard a door open and heard footsteps heading towards the back.

Kabir opened the boot. He was covered in blood. His eyes were red and his hair was dishevelled. He untied my legs, peeled off the tape on my mouth and took me out of the boot.

"Where's Madhav?" I asked with tears flowing down my cheeks.

"I killed him right in front of you. The bullet hit him right here." He kept his finger on my chest.

"Don't you dare touch me! I trusted you," I cried.

"I won't. Don't be worried, you are safe. You know why?"

He came close to me and whispered in my ears, "I don't like girls. I just like to sell them. Madhav was quite handsome but he knew too much about me. Sooner or later, he had to leave this world."

I could not believe that this cold-blooded killer was the same Kabir that I married a day ago.

"Just untie my hands and I'll show you what Madhav's sister can do!"

"So, you want to fight now, hah lady?"

He laughed with cruelty and untied my hands. I tried to slap him but he held my hands and slapped me. I fell a few metres away from him. I got up and lunged at him but he caught my throat and threw me back. I started shouting. "Help… help!"

We seemed to be in an isolated area and I prayed that someone would hear my cries of help.

"No one's going to hear you unless I'm unlucky. But I know my luck. It's not that bad," he smirked.

I bolted towards him and hit him in the face. That was unexpected. He got furious and was about to hit my face but he stopped and snarled, "Not on the face or I may lose some money."

He punched me in the stomach. I cursed in pain. I fell to the ground as he started laughing loudly. His every laugh filled me with energy. I felt something beside me. It was a heavy branch. I picked it up and without wasting any time, I hit Kabir's face with all my might. He fell down but I did not stop. Anger and fear had unleashed a beast in me and I continued hitting him till he became lifeless.

After a few seconds, I sat in front of him. His head was bleeding. And I was holding the bloody branch in my hand. I looked up at the sky and let out a loud scream. I felt relief from within. I knew I had done something which I should not have, but I was happy that I killed a man who had killed my brother. I was happy that I had killed a man who was selling women for money. I was happy that I had killed a demon. I took his pager and his wallet and ran to the car. I started driving. I wasn't sure whether what I had done was right or wrong, but I knew that I was safe.

I drove the car to the nearby police station. I parked my car. I was still holding that bloody branch in my hands. I opened the door and came out. The people present there were staring at me. Dragging the branch, I entered the police station and sat in front of a police officer. I did not see his face.

"I have killed my husband," I said. He stood up in surprise. A person came to me with a camera and mike. He looked like a reporter. I didn't care who he was.

"Ma'am, why did you kill him?" he asked.

"He was trying to sell me," I said and turned to the inspector and added. "I have evidence with me. You can let me go only if you feel what I did was not a crime."

"Ma'am, your name please?" the cameraman asked.

"Hey, let me do my work. You'll get all the information from our report. Till then you can wait outside," a policeman said.

"Sorry sir, but I won't disturb you. But can I sit here until she files the report?"

He handed a thousand-rupee note to the policeman. He did not say anything and allowed him to sit.

I described my entire ordeal in detail. I was kept behind bars and they offered me a government lawyer. For four days, I remained all alone in jail. There were some other women with me too. They tried to talk to me but I didn't share anything with them. I kept to myself wondering what my fate would be.

I came to know that Madhav was no more. The police found his body at Kabir's place. He had hidden his body in a fridge. Kabir's dead body was found near the place I had described. I came to know that the news had gone viral in the city but I wasn't sure what the impact was. Some reporters were trying to meet me and take my interview but the staff wasn't allowing them to. I regret that I didn't listen to Madhav. I was blaming myself for his demise.

"You'll be bailed by tomorrow," Meera came to meet me in jail. She was wearing a white sari. I couldn't hold back my tears.

"I'm sorry; it was all because of me. I should have listened to Madhav," I said in a broken voice.

"It wasn't your fault at all. I supported you too, so let's just stop the blame game. And I want to discuss something with you when you are back home."

Meera had hired a lawyer to get me bail. Just after a few hearings, I was out on bail thanks to of the media. When I came out of jail there was a huge crowd waiting for me. As I walked towards the car, they started showering flowers over me. Some tried to throw a garland of flowers on me.

I could not understand what was happening. Why were the crowds present? Why were they greeting me with flowers? I was a murderer, wasn't I?

Meera opened the car door for me and let me in, before sitting beside me.

"What is going on?" I asked Meera.

"People think you are a hero. You killed the man who tried to sell you. They want a bravery award for you. Just look at them – they are cheering for you. You have set an example and they are all here for you. You've made me proud today, Maya."

The car took us home. There was a crowd there as well. Some news reporters were ready with cameras. Meera didn't allow the driver to stop the car and told him to take the car inside. I felt as though Madhav would come out any moment to greet us. I began to falter as a different kind of fear was running in my blood. Meera caught my hand and helped me into the house.

"You can go to your room and get freshened up. I need to talk to you," Meera said. I could see the urgency on her face. It was evident that she had an important matter to address.

"Meera, I'm really very tired. Is it that important? I need some rest. I can't think straight. Hope you understand."

"I'm sorry. I should have thought about you. Go and sleep. We'll talk tomorrow."

She smiled. I smiled back and went back upstairs.

Every corner of the house reminded me of Madhav. He had been the elder brother I had never had. I reached my room and I could see Madhav standing in front of the door. He was holding a plate and he knocked on the door like he always did. I could see myself opening the door.

> "At least look up to see who's at the door, Maya."
>
> I didn't turn back and said, "It could only be you, Madhav. There's only one person who wakes me up so early."
>
> "Ya, that's because I want you to have breakfast. Now go and brush your teeth."
>
> I walked to the bathroom knowing he wasn't going to let me sleep.
>
> "Come fast Maya, have your breakfast," Madhav called

out to me. He offered me a plateful of sprouts. Madhav always brought me breakfast that I didn't like.

"Madhav, you know that I don't like sprouts," I said.

Madhav turned to me and said, "I know you don't like them but they are good for your health. Just come here and sit."

He took a spoonful of sprouts and said, "Just close your eyes and think that you are eating a dosa," I did as he said. And he put a spoon of sprouts into my mouth.

"But they don't taste like a dosa, Madhav."

"Ya, I know but just remember a dosa's taste in your mind. Just a few more spoons."

"Now, I'm full, I can't have any more. Please." I protested.

"Just close your eyes as I said. This one is last for sure. Just close your eyes." I closed my eyes.

"This tastes bad, Madhav. This is the last time…" and I opened my eyes.

There was no one in the room. No sprouts, no plate, no Madhav. I stood alone. Madhav was no more and it had been a figment of my imagination. I broke down and cried my heart out till I fell into a deep slumber.

A knock on the door woke me up the next morning. I was still in the previous day's clothes. I opened the door and Meera stood there holding a tray of food.

"Sorry, I thought you would be ready. Meera, please get ready and have your breakfast. I told you yesterday that I need to talk to you. Please get ready."

Meera kept the tray on the bedside table and went out without saying anything else. What could be so important? I didn't give it much thought and had my bath. I opened my wardrobe. I was a widow and had to wear a white sari.

So, I picked one with a green border. I wore it and went downstairs. I saw some people waiting in the hall. Everyone looked up at me. They stood up and started clapping when they saw me. It was an awkward situation. I went to Meera and stood next to her. Meera introduced me to them one by one. All of them were dressed in white. I guessed they were workers of the party. For a few seconds, there was pin-drop silence.

"Mayaben, I suppose you know why we are here," one of them said.

"The fact is that I didn't get much time to talk to her. Yesterday she wasn't feeling well so I allowed her to rest," Meera said before I could say anything.

"You did the right thing. She needed the rest. I guess she's fine now and we can talk to her," another one said.

"Look Mayaben, we all know that you have gone through a very difficult time. The way you fought back was inspirational. The country needs a courageous lady like you. We want you to join the party."

I was stunned. Why were they offering me such a role? Did I deserve such an opportunity? I didn't know anything about politics. I made up my mind to say no. But I stopped myself and decided not to say anything at that moment. I just joined my hands and got up from my place without giving them an answer.

"Don't worry. I'll talk to her. You guys please go. She needs some time I guess," Meera murmured.

I went upstairs to my room. I went to the balcony and saw all the men leaving in their cars. One of them looked at me and smiled with joined hands. I gave a little smile in return. I looked up at the sky. There were birds chirping. I closed my eyes listening to the soothing sounds of nature. I felt a sense of calm even though Madhav's loss was still there somewhere deep in me.

Meera came and stood quietly beside me.

"Sorry, Meera, I didn't know you were here," I said as I opened my eyes.

"Don't worry. I know why you are here. I know whenever you feel lonely or sad you come here. Have you come to a decision about joining politics?"

"Meera, you know I can't do that. I don't even know the basics of politics. I don't want to do anything right now. I just want some peace. And I know politics would never give me that. Please tell them I'm not ready."

"You know what, Maya, even your brother was saying the same thing about joining politics when he was offered the place. But my dad convinced him. I don't know what he did or said but he was sure that he would do well in this field. He trusted Madhav as I trust you now."

"Meera, please don't force me. I know I can't do that."

"It will be your decision. I won't force you. I'm just saying that I trust you. You can do anything. I know that when you joined our shop, the sales and profits increased. That proves you are better than Madhav."

"I can't be better than Madhav."

"I can't say anything about that at this stage, but do you know what was Madhav's last wish? To achieve victory. He gave his best to lead the party to the top. And now other party members think that the party won't survive without him. Elections are around the corner and they don't have a leader to represent them," she said.

"But, I'm not their leader."

"Just come with me." Meera held my wrist and took me with her. She switched on the television. My name was being discussed on a news channel. She switched to another one. I was on it. Then another which had my story. I seemed to be the subject of every channel.

"See, it's clear you are in the spotlight. The people have been inspired by you and by how you faced such an ordeal. They see you as a potential leader. Look at yourself through their eyes. Anyway, I will wait for your answer. It is your decision in the end. Just keep Madhav's dream in your mind. And you might not believe in yourself, but I know you are better than Madhav."

She went back downstairs. I returned to the balcony. I closed my eyes only to see Madhav's smiling face. I was horrified. I ran to my room. I was still blaming myself for his loss. I had loved Kabir. I still couldn't believe the things he had done to me. I had lost my brother and was a widow as well. How many women were out there suffering like me? Many of them wouldn't even have the courage to fight back. There were many evil men like Kabir exploiting women for their greed. This was a chance to show them their place. I realized that I had forgotten all about my daughters. I hadn't even talked to them. I owed it to them as well. I could do anything for them. I got up from the bed. I went to Meera and said, "Tell them Mayaben is coming."

6

Mayaben

It was my first day in office and I was clueless. They had appointed a person to help me learn the ropes. I was given some files to look at. Everything seemed to be in a mess. The party didn't seem to have an agenda. There was so much work to be done in a very short period of time. Someone entered the room as I was checking a file. I didn't look at him as my eyes were still on the file.

"So, you are the person sent to help me, right?"

"Yes, ma'am," the man replied. His voice sounded strangely familiar to me. I looked up at once. To my surprise, it was none other than Nayan. Though it had been years since I had last seen him, I knew I wasn't wrong. He had been my first love. And the first boy who had ditched me and left me in a terrible position.

He was still the same but he was just a stranger to me now.

"Oh, Maya? It is you. You are Mayaben? Of course, I knew that you were the new face of the party but I had no idea that it was you," he said before I could react.

"Nayan, I don't think I can work with you. You can leave," I said calmly.

"But Maya…"

I turned to my work and again told him, "It's better that you address me as 'ma'am'. I don't want a jerk like you in my office. So, just leave. Else I have to call the guards."

I started checking my files again. I could hear the sound of doors opening and closing. I dropped the pen, closed my eyes and sighed. It seemed like I could never get rid of my past. Why did he come back to my life, making me relive that terrible period?

"Why did you send him back?" Meera said, walking in. She was furious.

"Meera, you don't know him…" I replied.

"I don't want to know what he has to do with your past."

She was still angry but she tried to control her anger and sighed.

"Look Maya, you have to deal with your past. You just can't run away from it. If you know him from your past, you also must know how intelligent he is. Maya, we are running out of time. Elections are coming and there is no way I'm going to lose. I want to fulfil Madhav's dream. And I guess you want the same. Please get him back and deal with your past."

It was kind of emotional blackmail on her part, but she was right. I had to deal with my past. My silence worried her and she went out without saying anything more. I pondered about calling him back.

Meera was right. He had always been a topper along with me. And I knew he was perfect for the job. He had charm and charisma and was street smart as well. I rummaged for his CV that had been kept on the table. As I went through his list of qualifications, I knew I had to call him back immediately. I called a peon.

He came with a gift in his hands and kept it on my table and said "Meera ma'am has sent this for you."

"Okay, leave it here. You go and see whether that man is still there or has he left? If he's there, call him back."

"I guess he's in the waiting area. Meera ma'am had told him to wait outside. I'll send him in."

He went out and I looked at the gift. I opened it and found a brand new mobile phone. I knew nothing about mobile phones. I pressed a switch on the phone but it was locked. I tried a few more buttons but nothing worked. In a few minutes Nayan entered the cabin again.

"Yes ma'am?"

"Please come in. I'm sorry for my behaviour. But I guess according to Meera you are the best candidate for this job. And I'm giving you a chance."

I was feeling rather awkward. I told him to leave and contact Meera for further instructions. I again started trying to unlock the phone.

"Wait!" I called out to him.

Nayan turned back and I added, "Do you know how to unlock this phone?"

"I guess. Just let me check."

He asked for the phone and I handed it to him. In a second he unlocked it and even taught me how to use it.

"Thank you, Nayan."

"No ma'am, please don't say thank you."

"Please don't call me 'ma'am'. That sounds awkward. It would be better for you to call me Maya. And that doesn't mean anything okay. We are just friends."

He sighed and just smiled. It would not be easy to work together as memories of the past would haunt us, but we had to make it work for the sake of the party.

The pressure of the elections was so severe that we forgot we had dated in the past. As time passed, we grew comfortable in each other's presence. We were experts and worked tirelessly preparing the speeches, party agenda and campaigns. Meera was waiting for the right time to get me in the public spotlight. We organized a huge rally. Meera was the one to lead. Nayan and I prepared a beautiful speech for her. Meera read out the speech and came to me.

"This is just superb. You two are great," Meera beamed.

"Ma'am, it was all done by Maya. I haven't written a single word. And it was the first draft. She is too good. I just wrote for the other party members. Your speech is exclusively written by Maya," Nayan said.

"Well, it's quite impressive. Anyway, tomorrow you are coming with me to the rally, both of you."

We weren't prepared but it was her order. All the party members were happy with our work. Putting their trust in three new members was not easy but they believed in us. Because I joined the party, our major focus was on saving the girl child and girl power. The rally was to begin in the morning at 9 a.m. We didn't sleep a wink that night as we prepared for the next day. It was also evident that people were coming to have a glimpse of me as I was a household name by then. My foray into politics was a topic that was being discussed in all the channels.

"Maya, come with me," Meera called me.

"But Meera, we have a lot of pending work. I can't leave it like that. We are running short of time," I said.

"Nayan will take care of it. You have to stay with me," she said.

"Maya, don't worry. I'll manage everything. You just go with ma'am," Nayan reassured me.

I gave a thumbs up and left. Meera took me with her to a ladies' salon. What was I supposed to do there?

"Meera, I don't think you need me here," I said but she did not reply. She called out to one of the staff members and gave her a bag.

"Please get us ready quickly."

"Why do I need to get ready, Meera?"

"People are coming to see you. And I want you to look perfect. Don't worry it's just a plain white sari with some border work that will suit you. And please don't argue. We don't have much time," she said and started giving the attendant instructions. Then she went to get ready.

They were applying many things on my face. They experimented with various hairstyles as well. I was losing my patience as well as my temper. I was constantly thinking of all the work I had left midway. We took two hours to get ready. We ran to the car and sped back. Both of us were tense. People had already arrived. Nayan had managed everything well. We covered our faces and Meera told the driver to take the car to the back stage. I could see the banners and posters with my face everywhere. People were wearing t-shirts with my name and pictures. Some were holding slogans in support of me.

"Thank god you guys have arrived. I was so tense. People were out there waiting for you both. I had to start the programme," Nayan said as soon as we arrived.

Then he turned to Meera and added, "Meera, are you ready with your speech?"

She just nodded her head.

"Cool, next is your speech, Meera. And take Maya with you on stage. Just introduce her and tell the people that she is a party member now. Best of luck, Meera. And both of you are looking super cool," Nayan said everything in one breath and ran off to attend to something else.

The plan was to introduce me at this point of time. I felt like everyone knew me already though. I had seen my posters and slogans in their hands. Nayan went on the stage and announced our names. My heartbeats increased in tempo.

Meera held my hand and took me with her. We looked at each other and shared a smile. That boosted some confidence in us. We both walked while holding each other's hands. Meera's hair was tied in a long ponytail while mine was done up in a chignon bun. We masked our fear with big smiles on our faces. We stepped onto the stage and people went gaga. I could hear my name everywhere. It was a very new experience for me. I really wondered what expectations they had from me.

Meera and I were still holding hands. We walked to a mike and Meera took one in her hand and was about to speak. Suddenly she looked at me and said, "Why don't you say something?"

She had spoken into the mike and everyone started cheering. I had no option but to take the mike. I had no idea what to say. I sighed and closed my eyes. I made up my mind to be as strong as I could. I wanted to fulfil my brother's dream. Now it wasn't the only thing I wanted to do by joining the party. I could feel what people wanted from me. I took a deep breath and opened my eyes wide. People started cheering louder than before. I could hear them chanting my name, "Mayaben… Mayaben…"

I wiped the tears that had filled my eyes and raised my hand. They became quiet. I could hear the sound of the wind blowing. I brought the mike close to my face and began the speech.

"Namaste Gujarat…" Again a loud cheer followed by silence.

"I know you have a lot of expectations from me but I can't fight every devil out there."

People started murmuring but I continued,

"But I can teach you how to fight by yourselves. I was lucky that I managed to get something in my hands to save myself. Every girl in this country won't be that lucky. Yes, I killed my husband…"

After a round of applause. I continued, "I killed him because I wanted to save myself. I killed him to save every girl in our country. Yes, I'm a killer when it comes to protecting myself. Do you want your girls to be safe? Do you want your girls to go out alone without any fear? I'll teach you that. Our party will teach you that. Meera and I have lost our husbands but still we are together. Together we can change the world. It's not only about increasing a girl's strength or power. It's also about changing the mentality of every man. Until and unless, his mind is free of all the rubbish, we won't win. Our fight is against the regressive thoughts, not against men. And we need men to support us in our fight. Men and women together can change many things. Education is the one thing that will bring major change. I want every Indian to be educated and well-mannered so that he can stay away from such thoughts. I want every man to respect women."

People started clapping.

"Let's change the world from a man's world to a human being's world. I joined politics to fulfil my brother's dream. And truly speaking that was the only agenda. But seeing the huge crowd present over here has made me realize what real politics should be. It should not be to fulfil your personal agenda; it's all about fulfilling people's agenda. Now my life is for you people. I'll live for you and will make sure your life's agenda is fulfilled. I'll make sure that your girls can go out without any fear. I'll make sure that all the crooks get punished. I'll make every girl strong enough to fight back even if they don't have any weapon in their hands. Let's be united. Let's fight together. Let's make our country liveable. Let's breathe without any fear. Namaste! See you soon at the polling booth!"

I gave the mike to Nayan and everyone started cheering. The applause was deafening. I went back and took my place next to

Meera. She held my hand and smiled at me. I could feel her pride. That day the rally was successful and everyone was on cloud nine.

We gathered for a post-rally meeting later on. A clear win seemed imminent. But as the party was new, we were afraid that people might not trust us. So fingers were crossed. We all sat together and had a discussion about our future railies. My speech was the main attraction. We also discussed the loopholes in our agenda and decided to address those seriously. The meeting was about to get over but Meera had something on her mind.

"I guess we need to declare our CM candidate. That might boost our vote banks. If people know who the CM will be, they'll confidently vote for us."

Everyone agreed but a name was yet to be decided. Meera gave every member a chit to write down a candidate's name. In a few minutes the work was done. Nayan was ready with a piece of chalk. He started writing the names on the board. He picked up one and wrote Maya on the board. Second one was Maya again. Third, fourth… it seemed every chit had my name on it. So, he could write only one name and that was mine. He threw the chalk in the air with a smile. He didn't even pick every paper. A few were left in the jar. I had written Meera's name but that paper was not picked.

It was evident that I had to take the lead. We had many rallies and we worked 24x7. Nayan and I made a good team. Everyone's eyes were on us. They were satisfied that they had chosen the best man for the party. We had many rallies and as expected, presenting me as a leader helped the party. We finally won and I took oath as the new CM of Gujarat. Mayaben.

The journey from Maya to Mayaben hadn't been easy at all. In those few months I didn't even visit my daughters. The party decided to hide the truth from the public but I decided not to. I declared all my secrets one by one to the public. My life was like an open book for all to read. I had nothing to fear and nothing to hide.

I decided to visit my four daughters after a few victory rallies. I stood outside my old house after almost four years. Nothing had changed. My elder daughter recognized me and bolted towards me. And I guess the other three must have seen me on television or might have seen my photographs. They recognised me and hugged me. I was so overwhelmed that I hugged them tightly. I sat on the floor holding them close as tears of joy ran down my cheeks. I kissed them before getting up. Sameer was watching me from the door.

I went to Sameer and said, "How are you?"

"Four years! Did you even think about your girls in all these years? You disappeared from their lives, knowing fully well there was no one earning money in this house. You had abandoned them when they needed you the most!"

"Sameer, our daughters are listening. I don't think this is the right time to discuss this."

"Really? You want me to hide this from them. They already know that you weren't there when they needed their mother."

"I'm sorry Sameer, but I was going through a lot. Then there was so much to be done."

"Ya, more important than your daughters? Now you are the CM. How will you take care of them? Just leave all that... why are you here after all this time?"

I kept quiet for a minute, sighed and said, "Look, I have come here to tell you that I won't be able to come here often and I'm afraid that I won't be able to take care of them. I know you and Mom are going through a financial crisis. I'll send you half my salary so that you can look after them, and our daughters can live well."

"Oh, so you are here to buy us?"

I tried to interrupt him but he did not stop.

"So, what would be your salary? Around a lakh rupees? So I would get fifty thousand every month. But would that be enough to buy a mother for my daughters? I thought you were here to take us to the CM's house with you. But I was wrong."

"Ya, I can do that too. I can take our daughters with me."

"What about me and Mom?"

"Sameer, we are divorced. As a CM it can damage my reputation. I can take Mom and our daughters with me but not you."

"Look Maya, I'm going to be very clear. It'll be all or none at all. It's your choice and don't you dare send any money. If you care for your daughters then take them with you, along with Mom and I. Otherwise you may leave."

I didn't know how to react at that point of time. I was sure this was the last visit to this house for me. I took out my sunglasses from the purse and put them on to hide my tear-filled eyes. I got up and started walking towards the gate.

I could see that my younger daughter was eager to run to me but my eldest one stopped her. I could see the anger in her eyes. It was clear that she would never forgive me.

I was in a position where I could have easily taken them. But I didn't want to hurt anybody. I knew that I wouldn't be able to give them time. And I couldn't possibly stay with my ex-husband. I had to make a choice between my personal life and the position I held. I consoled myself that they at least had their father and grandmother to love them. It was love that they needed first and foremost. I left with a heavy heart.

7

The Insider

Leaving my daughters with Sameer was very difficult for me. I knew they would not be taken care of well. Sameer was still jobless. So I told Nayan to take care of my family anonymously. They weren't accepting any assistance from me so I raised some fake donors to give them money every month. I used to give half my salary and they used to donate the money to them. However, that made Sameer only more dependent and he never worked after that. I know I shouldn't have given him money but I could not bear the thought of my daughters going to bed with empty stomachs. I had no option.

I also arranged for some companies to give him a job. However, he could never stick to a place and would leave after a couple of months. It was an endless cycle. Finally I gave up and began to shift my focus on my political career. We started working on saving the girl child. I opened self-defence academies in the city at different places where women would get free training.

We also focused on education. Meera helped me a lot. Educating men was equally important. We introduced the new subject of human relations in the curriculum where we majorly focused on value for human and human psychology. Equality between men and women was also discussed in detail. Soon we could see positive changes in the attitude of boys as well as men. We were getting a good response.

We opened new government schools with the latest facilities

and technologies and they soon became at par with the private schools.

We also made sure that the anti-social elements were punished. All complaints and cases were dealt with urgency and the perpetrators were put behind bars. We appointed a committee to look after such criminals and make sure that they get punished. Earlier Gujarat was the safest state to live in, and we needed to bring back that glory.

"Meera, I guess we are still missing something."

"Maya, we are now a criminal-free state. I think we have dealt with everything."

"I don't know why but it feels like we have not got to the bottom of it. The last criminal was saying that he has a boss, and I guess that boss is still alive."

"Maya, don't worry. He just said it to hide the truth. I guess he's the one behind everything."

"I don't know, but let's hope you are right."

We were sitting at our office and Meera was sitting opposite me. The CM's office was new, and had been designed by a good architect. Everything had been taken care of by Nayan. I preferred greenery so it was designed in such a manner that allowed a good view of the garden outside. I got up to take a look when suddenly a bullet burst through the windowpane and went past my ear. I sat down in shock and looked at Meera. We both instinctively lay down on the floor. I heard more bullets being fired, hitting the furniture and papers on my desk.

I could hear the commotion outside as the guards were trying to catch the perpetrator. There was a heavy exchange of fire. A few guards came in and whisked us away to safety.

Everything had happened all of a sudden. I was shaken. Few days ago I was telling Meera that we didn't require so much security because the people loved us. But Meera had been insistent. Thank god I did not refuse her. But the question was who was trying to kill me?

"I guess it's the opposition party."

Meera brought me out of my thoughts.

"Meera, we had kept this place as secure as possible. And it was a secret. And there's no chance that anybody from outside could enter the premises. We have such tight security. It seems like an inside job."

"Some outsiders must have come to know about it through the staff. I truly think it's the opposition party."

"I really doubt it," I said, pondering.

A guard asked for permission to enter the room.

"Ma'am, we could not catch the person. We followed him but he disappeared and there is no sign of him. Sorry, ma'am."

"No issues. Did you find anything else?"

He held up a packet with a white cloth inside and said, "We found this handkerchief behind that window."

He pointed out a small window in the corner where I kept a flower pot.

"Please get that cloth out of the bag," I said.

"Ma'am, we should not do that. This is the only proof. We should send it to the forensic lab."

"Do as I say. I think I know whose handkerchief that is."

"Whose?" Meera asked curiously.

The guard took out the cloth and held it out. I went near to get a closer view. I observed it carefully. I had guessed correctly.

"Did you find the guy?" Meera asked.

"No, I don't think it is his," I lied and told the guard to put it back in a bag and told him to not to share the news with the media.

"But ma'am, if we send this to the forensic lab, the media will come to know about it."

"Then don't send it."

"But why?" Meera asked and then looked around. She turned to the guard.

"Please leave. I'll tell you what to do with the handkerchief."

She turned to me after he left the room and said, "Maya, we have to find that bastard. He tried to kill you."

"Meera, please I don't want any *tamasha*. People love me. They might get angry and I'm afraid riots may take place. Let's keep it low. We will beef up security."

"You are not going to listen to me. Just do what you want."

Meera left the room in a huff.

I had identified the handkerchief's owner. I didn't tell Meera because I knew who he was. I wanted to talk to him first. I told the security to get the car ready and gave the driver an address. He dropped me off.

Nayan opened the door and was shocked to see me there. He did not move for a second and then realized that he hadn't welcomed me. He asked me to come in and sit. I guess there was no one else in the house.

"How are you? I heard that you were shot at," he said.

"Oh, so you got the news. I wonder how since no one knows about it."

"What do you mean?"

I didn't answer him and took out a gun from my purse. I kept it on the table and said "There you go. No one's here. It'll be easy to kill me now."

He pretended to be shocked by my behaviour.

"What are you saying, Maya? You think I was the one who tried to kill you? You are wrong. This is a misunderstanding," he said, wiping off the sweat from his forehead.

"Then why the hell was your handkerchief lying below my window, Nayan?" I shouted at him and threw the handkerchief on his desk.

Nayan got scared. Fear was clearly visible on his face. I did not stop there and said, "We trusted you. I believed that you were loyal to me… to the party. But I was wrong. I don't know why I trusted you. You have betrayed me earlier. Why did I trust you?" I sighed and went back to the sofa.

"Look Nayan, I won't do anything to you. Just tell me why did you do it?"

"Maya, believe me. I didn't do anything. I don't have anything to say. If you trust me you have to believe that I haven't done anything."

"Liar! Why do you men always lie? We trusted you but you betrayed us. Just tell me the reason. I won't leave until you do."

"Maya, I said I have nothing to do with that. Please believe me, otherwise just leave."

"Isn't it your handkerchief?" I screamed.

"Look Maya, I accept that the handkerchief is mine. But I didn't try to kill you."

I stood up and slapped him as hard as I could.

"Don't you dare fool me again, Nayan. I regret appointing you as my PA. I thought you would be loyal to your job at least. But I was all wrong. I'm afraid that you never loved me. It was all just for fun."

"Don't you dare question my love! It was as pure then as it is now," he said earnestly.

He still loved me? That was not acceptable. I had moved on and why the hell should I believe him?

"Don't you dare say that again. Tell me one thing, if you love me then why did you try to kill me?" I said in rage and held his shirt's collar.

He held my hands and said, "Maya, please listen to me. My handkerchief was there because I love you. You might have forgotten me, but I couldn't move on. You think I ditched you in the past. It's not true. My parents knew the truth about us. They sent me to another state for further studies to keep us apart. After completing my studies, I went back to your house. There I came to know that you were married. I did not want to disrupt your life by telling you that I still loved you."

I sat down on the sofa in a daze. He sat on the floor, held my hands and continued.

"Maya, I ran far away from your life. I did not contact you. I'm still unmarried because I thought one day you'll come back into my life. And see God gave me a chance to be back in your life."

He stood up and started walking to the window. I was wiping my tears still in confusion.

"Maya, you want to know what my handkerchief was doing at the window?" he sighed and without waiting for me to say anything, continued.

"I used to watch you work from that window. I wanted to catch a glimpse of your face. To wipe off the sweat running down my face,

I took out my handkerchief. But I must have dropped it. You were looking so elegant that I could not take my eyes off you."

"Soon after that you stood up and started walking towards the window, so I ran away leaving the hanky behind."

He turned back and came back to me and sat on the floor. My first love was sitting in front of me. He looked at me and said, "I still love you, Maya. I want to spend my life with you. I never dared to say that to you but now you've given me hope."

I looked into his teary eyes. I got up and walked a few steps away from him. I wiped away my tears. I did not have any feelings for him. I cared because he was my employee and because I believed he was a good friend.

"I'm sorry that I didn't trust you, Nayan. Just don't tell anyone that I was here. But I'll find the person soon. Till then you have to help me. After that you will be free to get another job."

I walked out without another word. I did not have any feelings for him and after knowing his feelings, I couldn't work with him. So I took the decision and walked out of his house.

If it wasn't him then who could it be? I did not have a clue. I needed to focus on my duties as the CM so I gave Nayan the responsibility to find the attacker. We never discussed that at the office and made sure no one else knew about our operation. We had checked all the CCTV cameras in the premises. We got a small glimpse of the attacker's face but it was not clear enough to identify the person. It was very difficult for us to find him. Few days later Nayan came with his laptop to the office.

"Maya, I got something."

He played the same footage in front of me.

"We have seen this a thousand times, Nayan. Please come to the point. I have work to do."

"Just hold on for a second or two," he insisted. He paused the video at one point and zoomed it. He focused on the attacker's wrist. He had a tattoo on his hand. It was Lord Shiva's tattoo.

"I feel like I have seen that tattoo somewhere, but I don't remember where," I said thinking hard.

"I know who he is. I tried to contact him but he's not reachable. I think he's underground right now but we will find him."

He was sure about the identity of the man.

"But who is he?"

"You remember when we were campaigning, we gave this man the responsibility to handle the crowd. He was a bouncer. Even at that time you noticed his Shiva tattoo. That's him."

"Oh! That guard, his name was…ummm… I think it was Vishnu. I can't believe he is the one behind the attack. But the main question is whom did he do it for?"

"I have asked for his call history. We should be able to get a clue."

We needed to find out the identity of the mastermind. Nayan was already on it. There was another thing that had been nagging me. According to Nayan, Kabir had a boss. Could it be the same person behind this attack?

One thing we were sure about though, and that was we were closing in to identify the attacker. I told him not to tell anybody else about our investigation. We didn't know whom we could trust. I went back home after handing over the work.

Meera opened the door.

"How was the day?"

"Nothing much, as usual."

"So, have you found the man?"

"Who?"

"The attacker? Have you forgotten?"

"Ya, I had forgotten him. You know how hard we are working for the development of government schools. We hardly got any time to investigate the matter," I lied.

"But we have to search for him. Why don't you hand it over to someone? Someone like Nayan."

I was shocked. Why did she take his name? Was it just a coincidence?

"I think you are right. I'll ask him tomorrow. But tomorrow will be too soon. Let me just finish this school project first," I stepped towards my room.

A thought came to my mind and I stopped and turned back to Meera and added, "Why don't you handle that case?"

"I tried to handle this case and look what I found."

She took out Nayan's handkerchief. I was shocked.

"Why are you doing this, Maya? You know the attacker then why are you shielding him? Just put that bloody bastard behind bars."

I sighed and said, "Meera, mind your language. I know what I'm doing."

"I guess you have feelings for him, right? I knew it," Meera retorted.

I closed my eyes to control my anger and took a deep breath and said, "Meera, I don't want to explain anything. You better let me do my work."

I did not answer her but went straight up. She cared for me. I thought of sharing the truth with her but I don't know why I decided not to. I went to my room and sat on the bed. I was tired. It had been a long day.

I went out to the balcony where Madhav and I used to chat. I could not see the greenery around our house clearly but the sound of the wind passing through the leaves was very comforting. I closed my eyes and took a deep breath. I could hear only nature's sounds, and they poured some life into me.

"Please, please help me, Madhav. I'm all alone. Help me to identify the person. I don't have any bad intentions. Show me the right path, Madhav."

A single drop of rain made me open my eyes. Maybe that was the sign that Madhav was still there with me. I was sure he was one of the twinkling stars in the night sky and was looking down at me. I touched the single drop of rain with my finger. I looked up at the sky. It was getting windier. I felt it was a sign that all my problems would be solved.

Early next morning Meera woke me up and told me to get ready. She informed me that we were having a meeting with the Andhra Pradesh CM. They had liked our transformation of government schools and wanted to discuss the strategies.

"I had to call Nayan. He has all the material for the presentation. And don't worry I won't discuss anything about last night," she assured me.

"I'll be ready in a few minutes. If I'm not wrong our flight is at eight," I confirmed.

"Yes it is. You just get ready. Nayan will be here any moment," saying that Meera went out. I wanted to call Nayan to know whether he had managed to retrieve the call history of Vishnu's phone but since he was coming home I thought I'd ask him later. I got ready in no time and went downstairs.

Nayan was already there sitting on a sofa. He had been offered some fruits. When I entered, he stood up. I could feel that he was uncomfortable and he looked stressed. Meera was sitting on a chair opposite him. As I entered Meera told me that she'd get some water for both of us. I got an opportunity to talk about the culprit.

"So, did you find him?"

He didn't hear me and seemed lost in his thoughts. Physically he was present here but mentally he was somewhere else. I shook him by his shoulder and said, "What happened? Are you listening?"

"You should not live here, Maya. It's dangerous here," he held my shoulder and said. He was sweating profusely.

I shook off his hand.

"What the hell? Why are you behaving like this? I just asked you the name of the culprit."

"Yes Maya, I know the name and that's why I'm telling you to leave the house. The person is from your house and it's none other than Mee—"

Before he could finish, someone sped past me with a knife. And before I could understand what was going on, the person thrust the knife into Nayan's stomach. He cried out in pain as blood began oozing out. I looked at the person in horror and to my shock it was Meera!

She pushed me back and I fell on the floor. She removed the knife from Nayan and pushed him aside. She seemed like a madwoman and her face was red with anger.

She went to Nayan and kicked him as hard as she could and then turned to me "I knew you guys were on to something. I thought of killing you both in Hyderabad and putting the blame on the opposition party. But no, you guys just wouldn't let it go!"

She started walking towards me.

"I did not want to kill Nayan but I had to because of you, Maya. I had no choice."

I was still lying on the floor in shock observing her. I saw that she was coming to kill me as well. I was sliding back. Suddenly my eyes fell on Nayan. He had managed to get up and had taken a shawl and wrapped it around his waist to stop the blood from flowing. Luck was on his side as the knife had missed puncturing his major organs. Meera noticed that I was looking at something behind her. She turned around but I managed to stop her midway.

"Why do you want to kill me?" I cried drawing her attention back to me.

"Why? Because you stole my husband from me. I always kept telling him that you would be trouble for our family but he did not listen to me. Instead he kept supporting you."

She kept on moving towards me as I slid backwards. Nayan was slowly inching towards Meera.

"But even you supported me. You forced me to join politics," I said.

"You are right. I made you join the party but you never had my support. I did it just because other party members were supporting you. You killed Kabir and you became a hero. And I thought it would be good if you joined the party so that our party would have an easy win. I had already planned to kill you after our win but decided to allow you to set the base and goals for me so that I could work with you and win people's hearts."

I ended up against a wall. She smiled at me and continued coming towards me.

"You know what, Maya? It was a dream for me to become the CM. The day Madhav was killed, I was sure to get entry into the party and I did. I was about to be announced as the new party face but then you had to go ahead and do something to hog all the attention. It worked out though and gave us a big win."

She reached me and brought her face close to mine and said, "But now we don't need you anymore."

"I have a feeling that Kabir was working for you. That means you killed Madhav just for the power and position. And now you are killing me for the same," I said before she could attack.

"Don't you dare say that. I loved him more than anything. I would have killed anybody for him but not him. My love for him was true."

She came close to my ears and whispered again, "Do you know who killed Madhav? It wasn't Kabir. It wasn't me either. Then who could it be? I guess I know."

She started laughing loudly and leaned towards me again to say the name. But before she could say anything, Nayan hit her head with a flower vase. She screamed in pain and tried to attack Nayan with the knife but in a few seconds, she slumped to the floor. I sprang up and checked her pulse.

"Nayan, she's alive. I guess we should take her to the hospital."

My eyes were on Meera and when I turned to Nayan, I found that he too had lost consciousness. I didn't know what to do. My brain wasn't working at all. It went blank. I gathered myself quickly and bolted outside. I called the guards and they came running towards me.

"Get them to the hospital," I said pointing my finger towards Meera and Nayan. I followed them in another car. I closed my eyes and prayed for their safety, keeping aside the wrongs they had done to me.

We reached the hospital in no time. People around us recognized me but I didn't care about that. I wanted to stay with them but because of the crowds I was advised to return home. I was tired of all the betrayals. I went to my room and closed it from inside. I used to keep a small idol of Lord Krishna. I took it out from my cupboard and held it in my palms. I closed my eyes and prayed for both of them. I went out to the terrace hoping that the breeze would calm me down. But there was no wind that night. It was a strangely quiet night and the familiar, comforting sounds of nature that brought me much solace were absent. I turned back and walked towards my room. The cry of a peacock suddenly hit my ears. I stopped and looked at it. Suddenly a breeze caressed my face and a few drops of rain fell on my head. I looked up at the sky. I could see the black clouds. The peacocks were welcoming the rain with their joyous cries. It soon began to rain heavily. I stood on the balcony getting drenched. I was a human too. I needed such refreshments in my life. And that day, particularly, I needed it desperately. I smiled and looked up at the sky and thanked God. How I needed that smile.

I felt as though both my right and left hands were missing. As I stood in the rain, I felt like the anger, pain, sadness, betrayal, and every other emotion were being washed out from me. I cried as hard as I could. The rain was hiding my tears and my screaming was drowned by the thunder. I went down on my knees for a few seconds. I got up and went inside and cleaned myself. I felt relaxed after letting everything out from me. Before I knew it, I fell into a deep slumber.

A phone call woke me up in the morning. It was the doctor. He informed me that both of them were out of danger. I thanked God and rushed to the hospital. It was early morning around five.

"You said they are out of danger, I want to meet them," I said to the doctor.

"Calm down, ma'am. I said they are out of danger but you can't meet them now. Nayan is well and he'll recover in a few days. But I'm afraid Meera…" he hesitantly said.

"What's wrong with her?"

"She's out of danger but has gone into a coma. And we don't know when she will come out of it. She received serious injuries in her head. We are lucky that she's out of danger. The swelling disappeared overnight and we have hope that she will come back soon too."

"Hope? If you are giving any false hope, please don't do that. And if not Meera I guess I could meet Nayan. I have to meet him even if you say no," I said.

"Ma'am, I guess your fear is right. We might not get Meera back. At this stage we can't say anything about her. We can only pray for her."

"She's just following her karma," I interrupted him.

"Whatever it is, please pray for her good. And about you meeting Nayan, since you have already made up your mind, there's nothing I can say that will make you change your mind. Just take care that he doesn't get stressed. That might affect him badly."

I nodded and went to his room. I opened the door and entered. The room temperature was low. The room smelt fresh. I must admit that I like hospital rooms because they are usually my favourite colour – white. Before Kabir died, I wasn't allowed to wear a white sari. After Kabir's death I have always been in white by choice. I looked at Nayan. His face was still the same. The sound of a door closing woke him up. He opened his eyes and looked at me.

"You look handsome in a beard," I said.

Despite the pain a smile came to his face. He grimaced.

"Don't move, don't move. You are not well yet," I smiled, held his hand and added, "I'm glad that you are fine."

"What about Meera?"

"She's in a coma. You hit her really hard," I smiled.

"She was about to kill you. What did you expect me to do?"

"I know."

"She was going to reveal a name but I was more concerned about your life so I just hit her on her head."

"Don't stress about it. She was about to name that mastermind who is behind the selling of girls in Gujarat. He's still hiding somewhere. But you don't need to worry right now."

"What will you do?"

"I have no option but to wait. We have tried everything to find him but we have not succeeded. Let's pray that Meera comes out of coma,"

"I didn't know that she was revealing the name of that man, but I'm glad that I saved you," Nayan held my hand.

It felt wrong and I slowly took my hand back. I got up from the stool and said, "Get well soon."

"Maya, I know you don't have any feelings for me. But I'll never forget you. Just one request…"

I didn't move until he finished. I didn't answer him. I wanted to hear his request but to say yes or no wasn't possible for me. I stood there facing the door.

He continued, "I respect that you don't want to be with me at all. But I can't live without you. If not as your PA, please retain me as your peon. I want to be with you. I promise it will be like I never had feelings for you. Just keep me with you."

I could hear his voice breaking. I gave it a thought and said, "Nayan, you won't be happy with me. You will always be in pain. I don't want this one-sided love to be a reason for your misery. You are just half a person… I can't bear that."

"You really think I'm half? Maya, I gave you my half years ago. And then you gave me your half. I still have your half with me. I know when you moved on, you let go of my half. So, technically you are half, not me. I was half before I met you but I have been complete since. And I don't want anything else from life."

"I learned to live my life that way, Nayan. Together, we would never be complete. It would always be one and a half. I know how to live with that. Would you be able to manage that? Because you will be in a lot of pain."

"You are right that we will not make two. But one and a half is better than one. What you are calling pain is pleasure for me. My life will be full only by seeing you. Please Maya, let me be with you."

I stood still, looking at the door. Nayan was the only person whom I could trust. I gave it a professional thought. He was brilliant at his job and we needed him. Without wasting much time I said, "Join as my PA as soon as you get released from the hospital." I did not look at him and left. That must have brought a smile to his face.

8

Kill to Save

Present

"Hey brother, how can I be..." Rajiv entered our room and saw that the CM was in our cabin. Soon after, a few security guards rushed into the room.

"Ma'am, he's my brother. Please let me meet him." We didn't expect a response but she raised her hand to stop them. They let him go and left the room. Rajiv bolted towards Maya. He fell over his legs and said, "Thank you, ma'am. I'll never forget this," he said, holding on tightly to her legs.

"Rajiv, get up," she said sternly. I looked at Mona. We were wondering how the CM knew his name. Our eyes turned back to them. Rajiv did not listen to her and was still at her feet.

"Rajiv!" She raised her voice and Rajiv immediately stood up. He came and stood next to me.

"How does she know you?" I whispered to him.

"Jigar, she's my mother-in-law," he whispered back.

"You are impossible. It's not the time to joke," I hissed at him.

"I can hear everything. No need to whisper," Maya said.

"Ma'am, sorry, but he always jokes even during serious situations."

She again raised her hand to get me to stop talking.

"He's right. I'm his mother-in-law. He's Misty's husband. You know Misty, right?"

I felt like I had heard that name somewhere but where? I thought hard and then recalled that she was the woman we had met in the morning. The one who was looking after her ailing father.

"Mona, she's the same woman that we met in the morning… in whose house you had hurt yourself," I whispered.

"But she was unmarried," she made a point.

"I don't understand why you guys are whispering?" Maya interrupted us and added, "She married your brother Rajiv months back. She's staying there to take care of her dad, my ex-husband, Sameer." We were flummoxed.

"I do understand why you guys are confused. You must be thinking that if she's my daughter, then why is she in such a condition? They refused to take my help. They also found the sources through which I was helping them. I kept on changing the sources but somehow they'd find out. People like your brother Sachin have been very helpful. I respect your brother.

"However, my daughters are not mine anymore. They hate me and that hurts me a lot. It wasn't my dream to become the CM. I was just fulfilling Madhav's dream. And when I stand for my people, I don't break their trust by leaving them."

She paused for a moment.

"Ma'am we respect you. We know you have done great work. But why do you want to kill your ex-husband? And what happened to Meera? Was she okay or not? Who was the mastermind?" I said.

"I guess it was Sameer. That's why she wants to kill him," Mona said thoughtfully.

"Yes, you are right. He was behind everything. It still has not sunk in. Usually I would send him behind bars, but now his eyes are on Misty. He has to die."

"I'll kill that bastard!" Rajiv screamed in anger. I have never seen him so furious. She was his wife after all and he must love her dearly. What a dark horse he was, pretending to flirt with that doctor, while being married all the while. I restrained myself from giving him a whack.

"No, you won't do anything. Sameer knows you. You have been there many times. He can harm you too. Thank god he doesn't know about your marriage, else he would have attacked you," Maya said.

"But he is in bed and I don't think he can harm anyone. I'm sure you are wrong. Misty is his daughter and she's the only one taking care of him. How can he possibly do that?"

"No, I'm not wrong. He had married me to sell me off abroad as well. But he couldn't do that as he was unable to shift overseas. He failed to get a job so I was saved. I always thought he didn't have any money since he didn't have a job. But I was wrong. He earns so much that he can buy a villa for himself. Living in penury was a cover for him so that no one would ever suspect him. I was a fool that I couldn't see that. He doesn't care about comfort and riches, so I don't understand the reason to be part of such an activity. Maybe he has a plan, I wouldn't know."

"There are some demons like him. They do it without any reason," a guy standing near the door spoke. We didn't even notice when he entered the room.

"Nayan, I think you are right. Some people do things without any reason. They are just evil," Maya said.

So this was Nayan. It felt like we had known him for years. I was trying to search for his love for Maya in his eyes. Maybe Mona was doing the same. He was tall at about six feet. He was wearing a yellow kurta, and his features were sharp and clean.

"Jigar..." Maya made me look at her and continued. "I know you have never done anything like this, but you have to do it."

"Why me? You have many people around you. There must be professional killers out there. Why me?"

"We had sent a killer to kill him, but you reached the house with your brother. I thought of asking your brother first, but then I thought of you. We don't have time. And professionals may reveal my name. You will keep it to yourself. And even if you do tell anyone, you will be implicated."

Mona and I looked at each other. We both were tense. I said, "I can't do that alone, I need someone like… Mona. She is very clever."

Maya sighed and smiled.

"She's in bed. She will not be able to walk for at least a fortnight."

"After that…" I said it with a smile pasted on my face.

"Okay. I agree that you need a partner."

That fake smile started converting into a real smile and she added, "Rajiv will be a better option, I guess. He's sharp too."

My jaw dropped. It was better to go alone.

"I think I'll manage alone. Misty's father may recognise him. So, why take the risk?" I said.

Rajiv was nodding his head in agreement. His face clearly said that he was equally not interested in killing anyone, especially his own father-in-law.

"I am not talking about this anymore. The two of you are going and that's final. We have wasted enough time," she said sternly and gave Nayan a look.

As Nayan gave someone outside a signal, the door opened and the guards burst in. One pulled me aside while another went over to Mona and pointed his gun at her head.

"No!" Rajiv shouted. We all looked at him. "What are you doing, brother? Your wife has a gun pointed at her head. Stop them!" he added.

"I know. That's why we have to go and kill that bastard," I said.

"Nayan will be keeping his eye on you. Best of luck."

She went outside with her other guards. I sat down on a chair and kept my hand on my forehead.

"Are you waiting for him to shoot me?" Mona said sobbing.

"Why are you standing like a statue? Just kill her so I can breathe!" I screamed at the guard. Mona started crying louder.

"Don't you feel she's irritating you? Just shoot her, damn it!" I cried out in frustration. I took a deep breath to calm my nerves.

"Look Mona, it's not that I don't care about you... I'm just frustrated. How can I kill someone?"

She started crying harder. I went and held her hands.

"Look at me, look at me," I shook her hands and made her look at me.

She controlled her tears and waited for me to talk.

I looked into her eyes and said, "This too shall pass. I'll be back soon. Just wait for me. I'm sorry that I shouted at you."

She stared at me for a few seconds and then looked at Rajiv.

"I doubt you guys will be back. But don't worry I'll send you your meals in jail," she said and again started crying.

Rajiv sat beside me and kept his head on my shoulder.

"I don't want to go to jail," he said in a trembling voice, his eyes filled with tears.

I didn't know how to console the two. I started crying too. All three of us were crying. The guard lost his patience and shouted.

"*Chu...p... niklo... chal tum dono niklo idhar se!*"

We stopped at once. Rajiv and I got up.

"Out!" he screamed.

We ran out of the room bumping straight into Nayan. He

gestured at us to follow him. I knew that we had to carry out the mission. We had no choice. Mona's life depended on it.

"Look, Rajiv, I'll help you but you must do the actual killing," I said, hiding my fears.

He folded his hands. "I have never even killed a cockroach, how on earth will I kill a human being, bhai? Please get me out of this. I want to have kids," he said.

"That's the future, bro; only if you're able to survive the present. I already have kids. Who'll look after them?" I made an excuse.

"I'm there. I'll take care of them," he said.

"You are such a moron."

"Same as you."

"Hey stop fighting like kids and sit inside the car," Nayan said when we reached Rajiv's car.

Rajiv was about to take the driving seat but I stopped him and tried to take his key. I never trusted his driving. He had caused many accidents in the past, so there was no chance of me sitting in his car if he was driving.

"Okay take it but I won't get in if you are driving," I said.

"And if you are driving, I won't sit in my own car," Rajiv said.

"Hey get in or else I'll shoot you," Nayan pointed a gun at me.

"Okay kill me, I don't care. I'll probably die anyway if I get into the car he will drive."

Without wasting any more time Nayan snatched the car keys from Rajiv's hands. He opened the door of the driving seat and sat down. I smiled at Rajiv and plonked into the front seat.

"So, where are we going?" I asked.

"To kill Sameer," Nayan said.

"We are not ready yet. Don't you think we need to be trained first?" Rajiv said.

"You are not going to kill him with a gun. I'll give you a knife. You don't need any training to use one," he said as we sped down the road.

"Do you like your job?" I dared to ask.

"Of course I do."

"But living with a person who doesn't love you back must be difficult," I said.

"So, Maya has told you everything," he sighed and added. "Love is a very confusing word. Why expect the person we love to love us back? It's a big world. There was a time when we both were in love with each other. Now times have changed. She moved on but I couldn't," he said.

"But still why is she not accepting you now?"

"That's her choice. I can't force her to love me back. See, you are married and what if somebody from your past that you have broken up with, comes to you and says that she loves you. What would you do?"

"I'll accept her proposal," Rajiv interrupted.

"I'm not asking you. So, Jigar, you won't leave your wife at any cost that's for sure. Likewise Maya is attached to her work, attached to her brother's dream, and attached to the people of India. She has broken up with me and I can't expect her to be with me," he said.

"But what about you, Nayan? You can't always live in pain."

"I'm not in pain. In fact I feel like I am very lucky. I know I could not get her love but I'm lucky that I can be with her and I can see her every day. What else do I need? I did not get married just to be with her. I could not think about anyone else other than her. She's a strong woman and has dealt with so many heartbreaks. She is still standing tall. I just wish I was like her. She's an inspiration."

"I don't know why but I can't believe you. You must be happy but you are equally sad as well."

"That pain is my happiness. I love to be with her all the time. Eventually that pain converts into happiness,"

"I would never understand that."

"You don't need to. I think we are about to reach our destination."

He parked the car in front of the same place we had come to with Sachin. The nervousness was clearly visible on our faces except for Nayan's. Nayan was calm and confident. He handed us a knife. It was eight in the evening and it was quite dark. We came out of the car.

"It's quite dark," Rajiv said.

"We know that. Just focus on your work."

"I'm doing that. The point is we don't even know how to attack someone even during the day, then how will we target one at night," Rajiv said.

I immediately turned back towards the car and said, "I think you are right. We should come back in the morning."

Nayan was walking just behind me and stopped me from moving further. He pressed a gun on my stomach. I knew what he wanted to say so I just turned back and murmured, "How many guns do you carry?"

He heard that and replied, "Enough to control you guys."

We had no option but to move ahead. We were walking slowly with our knees and backs bent. Nayan poked me with the gun again.

"What the hell do you want?" I murmured in anger.

"Why are you walking like a thief? Walk normally. Speak normally as I am doing," he said. Nayan was right and we both stood straight.

"I need to pee," Rajiv said.

"There's a washroom inside. After we finish our work you can use it," Nayan said.

"I don't think I can wait that long," he again made an excuse.

In reply Nayan pointed the gun at his belly. He did not argue and turned back. We reached the gate in no time. Rajiv opened it and it creaked loudly. How could I forget that the gate made such a loud sound? However, thankfully, we saw no movement at the door. Rajiv and I both looked at Nayan. He pointed the gun at us again and made us move ahead. I knocked on the door and waited for a response. No one opened the door. That brought a smile to our faces. After a few seconds, I knocked on the door again and waited for a few more seconds. No one came to the door.

"I think no one's at home," Rajiv said with a smile pasted on his face.

"Knock again!" Nayan was getting furious. I knocked on the door but with very little force.

"Haven't you been fed properly?" Nayan said and pushed me aside with his hands." He started knocking on the door loudly.

Rajiv and I both looked at each other. We were worried about the neighbours hearing the racket. But luckily no one came out. The door was not locked. Nayan pushed it open and we went in. There was no one in the sitting room.

"I told you there's no one inside," Rajiv said with a smile on his face. We both felt relaxed and sat on the sofa. Nayan went off to search the house.

"Thank god that Misty is not at home. What would I have told her?" Rajiv said.

"First of all, tell me when and why you got married to Misty?"

"You know that I had decided not to marry anyone. A year back Misty was appointed as a part time worker in my company. When I saw her for the first time, I wasn't attracted to her. Her work impressed me a lot though. She was quite witty and punctual. She had the solution to every problem. And one of my colleagues made me aware that I had started having feelings for her. I proposed to her and she told me that she loved me as well but did not want to get married because she had to take care of her dad. But as time passed we could not stay without each other. We decided to get married secretly a few months ago and stay separately."

"I was dying to live with her but we had no option. Her dad was strict and he did not like my frequent visits. I seriously hoped he would have been at home. I would have killed him as he's the villain of our relationship," he added.

"Unfortunately, he's not. But if you really wanted to kill him, why were you so afraid?" I asked.

"You can't make all your wishes come true. I don't have the guts to do some things. And I'm not a serial killer who can kill a person easily, am I?" he said.

In a few minutes, Nayan called me. He sounded tense. We assumed he must have found someone in the house. We ran out of the room and saw Nayan standing at the door of one of the bedrooms. He went inside and we followed him. We stopped at the door where he had been standing earlier. Rajiv and I saw a dead body lying on the bed. The body's face was facing downwards. His head was bloody and the bed clothes were soaked in blood. We began to sweat in fear. Nayan, however, seemed unfazed. He was observing the scene without any emotion on his face.

We moved closer to the body to see who it was. And to our surprise it was none other than Sameer, Misty's father. It seemed that someone had done our job for us! I was suddenly overwhelmed and wanted to throw up. I received a tight slap on my back.

"Don't you dare puke? Do you want to go to jail for a murder you didn't commit?"

I quickly gathered myself.

"Who could have done this?"

"I don't have any idea."

We were all wondering when I noticed a flower vase, covered with blood, lying in one corner of the room. I went close to it and was about to touch it, when Nayan pulled me back and gave me another slap. This time it was harder than the earlier one. I was furious and slapped him back as hard as I could.

"I know I should not touch it. But you could have said that even without slapping me," I raised my voice. Rajiv was standing behind Nayan and he was clapping silently behind him. I ignored him and added, "Look I know it's routine for you. We have never even seen a dead body, so what we are doing is natural. Just inform us and don't you dare to touch me again."

"Done? Now just stay put and let me do my work," he said like nothing had happened. I was so furious that I wanted to kill him with the same vase. He kneeled down and was observing the vase without touching it.

"Somebody hit him with this vase," Nayan said after a few seconds.

"Oh really? We didn't know that. Thank you for informing us," I said, smiling.

He ignored me. Rajiv pinched me from behind. I turned to him and he had one finger on his lips, telling me to keep quiet.

"You want me to stay mum? Don't you dare do that again."

I was furious and turned back to Nayan. He was now standing tall and looking down at me with an amused look. He seemed rather formidable with his muscles and stern face. He stared into my eyes and said, "We should leave now."

"Yes, but where's Misty?" Rajiv asked.

"She's your wife… you should know," I said in annoyance.

"What has happened to you, Jigar? I know she's my wife and that's why I'm asking for her. I know we are in a fix, but we have to find her. She might be in danger," Rajiv said, frowning.

"I think he's right. She must be in danger," Nayan said.

I sighed and controlled my anger.

"Have you checked the whole house?" I turned to Nayan. He shook his head. Without wasting much time, the three of us started searching for her in the rest of the house. Unfortunately, we couldn't find her anywhere.

"I guess we should leave now. One thing is for sure Misty is not at home," Nayan said.

"Why don't you try to call her?" I said and in the next second, he called her. We could hear the phone ring. We followed the directions and found the phone being charged in the same room in which the body was lying.

"She always does this. Now where will we find her?" Rajiv sat down, looking worried. I had never seen him so tense before.

"Everything will be fine. We'll find her, don't be worried," I said.

"She loved her father a lot. How will she react when she finds out he is dead? We did not stay together just because she wanted to take care of her father and wanted to stay with him. She'll be broken," he said as tears ran down his face.

"Rajiv, control your emotions. We have to leave now or else we will be caught," Nayan said.

"Yes, Nayan is right. We should go now."

"I'm not going anywhere until she comes home."

"Rajiv, she will come back soon. We have to leave the house. I promise we will find her," I tried to convince him and finally he agreed to go, though with a heavy heart. We took care to see that nobody spotted us while leaving. We knew this murder was going to be in the headlines the next day. I was glad that I was not the murderer. But if not us, then who could it be?

We went straight to Maya and told her about the whole incident. Maya was happy that her ex-husband was finally no more but was tense about her missing daughter, Misty. She hadn't met her for years but still loved her dearly. She would do anything to find her.

9

Together

Two days passed by but Misty was still missing. Everyone was tense. Maya used all her sources to find her, but to no avail. Now she was tired too. She had not slept for almost forty-eight hours. So hadn't Rajiv and Nayan. I took a few naps as Maya did not allow me to go back to Mona.

"Maya, you mustn't be so stressed. It's not good for you. In the daytime, you work for the public and at night you go out looking for Misty," Nayan said while we were at her house.

"We have to find her."

"Okay, tell me where can we find her? I'll go personally and look for her," Nayan raised his voice a bit in frustration.

He sighed and added, "Look Maya, we have asked her neighbours and the people who know her including her friends and family. No one knows where she is. We even checked her call history but didn't find any clue. So, just give me a clue about where we could find her," Nayan said.

"I guess you are right, Nayan. We are looking for her without a plan."

"That doesn't mean we would stop looking for her," Rajiv said sadly. "I'll find her even from beneath the earth if I have to."

"I'm afraid that Sameer might have sold her," Maya finally said the words that we had only been thinking so far.

"No, this cannot happen. Do anything to find her, please. I won't be able to live without her," Rajiv broke down.

"Yeah, we can't give up. I will find her wherever she is," Maya said and then added, "Jigar, I think you should go back to your wife. She needs you at this time. She must be worried about you. I think you should leave. Just call me if you find anything regarding Misty."

Maya then turned to Rajiv.

"Rajiv, I guess you should also leave. We haven't rested at all and to search for her we have to take some rest. Let's hope that she is fine wherever she is."

"I'm ready to stay if you need me," I said firmly.

"I think you are right, Maya. I know it would be hard for me to even sleep but we have to regain our energy to search for her. I'll meet you in the morning. Thank you for your support," Rajiv said.

Maya smiled at Rajiv and turned back, "I'll pick you up from the hospital if I require anything from you."

I just folded my hands and walked towards the car. Rajiv also left with me and I dropped him home. On the way to the hospital, I was all thinking about Maya and her life. She had suffered a lot in life. She lost every person she loved but was still standing tall and ruling the state.

Love is the most beautiful thing in this world, but at the same time, it has the capacity to kill you as well. Maya was a strong woman, surviving three attacks by the sword called Love.

She understood the emotions and feelings of the people around her. She took care of her daughters even after staying away from them. Her life was dedicated to the people. Of course, she had done some bad things, but only for a good cause.

I reached the hospital in no time. Mona was still sleeping. I was seeing her after two days. It wasn't like I had never stayed away from her, but this time I had missed her terribly. She looked so beautiful, sleeping peacefully. I went near her and held her hand. I could feel her warmth and I cried. A teardrop fell on her hand and she woke up. She kept her other hand on my face and lifted my face a little bit to have a clear view. I raised my eyes; she was smiling at me.

"Stop smiling," I said, wiping my tears.

"What do you expect from me? I'm seeing you cry for the first time," she said.

"So, that makes you happy?" I asked surprisingly.

"Arrey no baba, I'm happy because you're crying for me. So, the smile means everything is okay, I guess," she sighed.

"For you? Never… they just came out naturally," I teased her.

"Oh, so you must be crying because you killed someone. I've been watching the news. I know it wasn't easy." She was worried about me.

"Don't be tense about that. Your husband is not a killer."

"Then who? Rajiv?"

"No."

"Nayan, I guess."

"None of us. We do not know who did it, but he was dead before we reached," I explained.

"Misty must know about it," Mona said after giving it a thought.

"She's missing too."

"What? Then I think she must have killed her dad and run away," Mona said, rolling her eyes.

"Don't be silly. As Maya said, she loved her dad a lot. How could she do that? I'm afraid that Sameer has sold her. Maybe he had an altercation with the buyer over money and he killed Sameer."

"That's quite possible," she sighed.

"Or something else altogether, who knows?"

I kept my head in her lap and she stroked my hair. I was dead tired and got up and went to the sofa to catch a few winks.

A phone call woke me up. It was Nayan, "Hey Jigar, please watch the news and call me back."

He disconnected the call.

"Who was that?" Mona asked. I was still groggy so I ignored her.

"Please say something, Jigar. Who was it?"

She wasn't going to stop until I answered her.

"Nayan."

"What did he say?"

"Just to watch the news," I said in a sleepy voice.

"Then watch it. There must be something important."

"Five minutes, love. Just five minutes," I said, falling asleep again.

I could hear the television being switched on. I did not react and pretended to sleep. But I could clearly hear the voice of the news reader.

'Rajiv Prajapati has been arrested for killing his father-in-law. His wife is still missing. Police are saying that he might have killed his wife too.'

"What the hell?" I got up from the sofa with a start. That was beyond my imagination.

'Sources are saying that there were two more people with him. Police are searching for them…'

Without wasting any time, I called Nayan.

"What the hell is this? Maya told us that nothing would happen to us. What nonsense is this? Tell Maya to call me otherwise I'll go to the police and tell them everything. She'll be exposed," I threatened.

"Maya speaking. And Nayan is with me. Say what you want to."

Her voice was calm and steady. I lost my temper.

"Maya, you promised that we would be fine. He's my brother and he's behind bars. Not only that, they are searching for me and Nayan as well."

"Nothing will happen to you and Nayan."

Why was she always so overconfident? I know she'd do anything to save us but still, the media had more power than her in this country.

"Jigar, listen to me. Why don't you come here? We can think of something," Nayan said. I disconnected the call and looked at Mona. She just blinked her eyes and told me to go.

"Come back soon," she added as she waved goodbye.

I rushed to her house. Nayan greeted me at the entrance to the meeting room, where I found Maya staring outside through the glass façade, lost in thought. She seemed deeply engrossed in her thoughts. We took our seats in silence.

"So what should we do now? The police will catch us easily," I said uneasily.

She turned back with a smiling face.

"Nayan, do one thing, our trees need to be trimmed. Also, take care of the lawn. And please take care while you trim that neem tree. There are lots of birds living there," she said like it was a normal day. She was as cool as ice.

"I asked you something, Maya," I got frustrated. She looked at me and sighed.

"Nayan, switch on the television."

Why the hell was she acting so strangely? Nayan switched it on. The breaking news read: 'Soon Mayaben will be visiting the place of the murder. Is there any connection? Everything will be revealed soon.'

"You two are coming with me. Make sure you guys hide your faces. We are leaving in fifteen minutes," she said.

"But the reporters will be there," I protested.

"They won't be allowed."

She turned to Nayan and said, "Here are the uniforms of the security guards. Be quick and confident," she said and went upstairs.

"Where's she going?" I asked Nayan.

"To change. We are going to Misty's house."

"She always wears a white sari then why is she changing?"

He ignored my question and handed the uniforms to me.

"What?" I asked.

"Wear them."

"Are you nuts?"

He just took out his loaded gun. Without arguing I changed into the clothes. I was frustrated. Why were they doing this?

Was the criminal hiding there? Was she smarter than the CBI? Why was I stuck with them? My mind was flooded with questions. Nayan and I got ready in no time and went to the waiting room. Maya was sitting on the sofa, waiting for us.

I whispered to Nayan, "She hasn't changed her clothes I guess." Nayan ignored me. We stood in front of Maya.

"Take your guns," she instructed. Nayan brought two guns lying on the table in front of her. He handed over one to me.

"Is it a real one?" I asked only to get a glare from him.

"I got it, but I don't know how to use it, Nayan," I whispered.

"You don't need to; there will be other guards. We only have to pretend to be her guards. Don't worry," he said and smiled.

Soon, we were on our way. A few metres before the house we saw some reporters. Maya did not even look at them.

"You won't see any reporters or any other person other than us around her house. Even the neighbours have been shifted out for a few hours. Only a few police officers and security guards will be present. So don't be worried," Maya said from the backseat. I was sitting in front with Nayan. Her words managed to calm me down.

I was still hopeless about the identity of the killer. But I don't know why Maya was so confident. I tried to hold the gun like the guards and followed Maya. We entered the house and reached the place where the dead body had been lying earlier. The police had marked it with white chalk. The policemen were explaining the scene to Maya.

In a few minutes, she sent everyone out except me and Nayan. She looked around thoroughly but could not find anything new.

We came out of the house when we suddenly heard a loud sound. It sounded like something had fallen. The police who were waiting outside also heard it so all of us rushed inside. However, we found nothing. We came out but Maya remained at the main door. Suddenly, her eyes followed the staircase and she started climbing the stairs.

"Ma'am, it's a single-story building. It's just a terrace," one of the police officers said. "We have checked it."

But she ignored them. We followed her with the other police officers following us. We reached the terrace and were shocked to find Misty lying unconscious there. Maya sat beside her and put her head in her lap. She started tapping her cheeks while calling out her name, "Misty... Misty..."

Simultaneously, one policeman checked her pulse.

"She's still breathing. We should take her to the hospital," I said.

Without wasting time, we took her to the hospital. Soon, the news spread and made it to the headlines on all the channels. Maya decided to stay with her till she regained her senses. We waited the whole day. She finally came back to her senses in the evening.

"Maya..." Nayan called out when he saw that Misty was awake.

Maya was staring at a blank wall. Without wasting a second, she rushed towards Misty when she heard Nayan. She looked at her and held her hand. Misty opened her eyes and looked at her mother. She looked at her for a while and then burst into tears.

She clung on to Maya tightly as her body trembled with her sobs. Maya tried to control herself but when a mother meets her daughter after years, how could she control all the emotions pent up within her? She looked up at the fan as her tears silently ran down her cheeks.

Maya wiped away Misty's tears. Misty looked at her and cried out, "You did a good thing by leaving Dad, and Mom, but why did you leave us behind with him? He was a devil!"

"What happened?" Maya asked with a frown as she held her close.

A police officer took out his pen and started writing down her statement.

"I killed him, Mom, I killed him!" she cried before bursting into tears.

The police officer looked at Maya. He asked her in sign language whether to record her statement or not. Maya shook her head. She calmed her down and made Misty look at her.

"Tell me everything in detail," Maya said softly.

"Mom, he came with a client. He wanted to sell me to him. An African man. Dad said he was his friend. He had brought some special African juice and Dad asked me to have some of it. In a few minutes, I fainted. A few hours later, I woke up in my room. I had a terrible headache. I realized that there must have been something in that juice. I got up from the bed to look for Dad."

"I stopped short when I heard voices arguing. It was the black man with Dad. I heard every single word. Dad wanted more money and he was not ready to pay. He found that I wasn't very young so didn't want to pay more money for me. In the end, they agreed upon a sum and they came towards my room to take me, I suppose. I was numb with fear and didn't know what to do. I picked up a vase from the table and hid behind the door. As soon as I heard footsteps approaching the door, I hit the person who entered the room first as hard as I could with the vase. I assumed it was the client, but it was Dad.

"Dad tried to steady himself but could not and fell over the bed, hitting the edge. I dropped the vase on the floor. That black man saw what had happened and ran away. I tried to wake Dad up but he did not get up. I checked his pulse only to find that he was no more.

"I got terribly nervous and did not know what to do. I picked up the vase and kept it back. I was feeling guilty and was afraid of the police, so I decided to run away. But where? I was about to run out of the house when I heard voices. I ran upstairs to the terrace instead. I stayed hidden there for two days without food or water."

"The house was always full of people once the body was discovered, so I did not get a chance to run away from there. And I don't know when I fainted out of hunger and exhaustion. I'm still scared and don't know what to do, Mom."

Maya wiped away her tears and said, "Look, Misty, you don't have to be worried about it. You acted in self-defence. What you did was correct. Your father deserved to die. Some reporters want to meet you but you keep mum. I'll handle everything."

Maya looked at Nayan and gave him a sign. Nayan called a reporter inside. He came with a cameraman and entered the room. He looked at Maya and took her permission to start recording.

"So, how are you feeling, ma'am?" the reporter asked. Misty just gave a little smile and nodded her head.

"How did you reach the terrace?"

"Doctors have not allowed her to speak yet. You can ask questions and she will reply with 'yes' or 'no,'" Maya interrupted.

"Okay, did anybody send you to the terrace?"

She replied 'no'.

"Do you know the killer of your dad?"

She did not reply and started crying.

"Did that killer try to rape you?"

"What the hell are you asking?"

Maya got furious.

"Sorry, ma'am."

He turned back to Misty, "Was he killed by a knife?"

Misty again went blank. I could see the pain Misty was going through. Maya was feeling her pain as well. I was standing there just watching everything but could not do anything about it.

"Was that person from your home?"

She kept quiet.

"You have to answer, ma'am."

He was forcing her. Maya was about to stop him but before she could, Misty shouted.

"Yes, that person was from my family. And you know who killed him? His daughter Misty killed him. Yes, I killed him!"

Nayan stopped the camera and sent the reporter out. But it was too late. He had been live and everything was disclosed.

Maya screamed at her, "I told you not to speak or say anything. You've ruined everything!"

She sighed and then calmed herself. "Don't worry I know how to get you out of this. You just rest and close your eyes. You are Maya's daughter. You don't have to be scared of anyone."

She went to the window and waited there for five minutes. She told me to put it on the television. 'Daughter kills father' was the headlines broadcasted by all the channels. I looked at her and wondered how she would react.

She picked up the phone and called someone. "Bring him here."

We did not dare to question her. We were waiting eagerly for the person. Just after half an hour, a few men entered with a tall black man. He must have been the one who had come to buy Misty. Maya closed the door from inside. She held the man from his collar and dragged him to Misty.

"Was he the one?" she asked. Misty just nodded and started crying.

Maya slapped him and dragged him out of the hospital which was teeming with media persons. Nayan and I followed her. She stood in the front foyer holding the crook. She looked at Nayan and handed over the man to him. There was a huge crowd waiting for Maya. The reporters were given the front spaces. Maya folded her hands. Then she raised both her hands to calm the public. She was offered a mike by one of the reporters.

She sighed and said, "My daughter, Misty, has killed her dad. He was my ex-husband."

There was pin-drop silence. I could not believe that I was standing in front of such a huge crowd. Everybody present wanted to hear Maya's words. Everyone's eyes were on her.

"Yes, she did it. You heard right. You have always heard rumours that I was married twice. From my first marriage, I had four daughters. They weren't rumours. All of that was true. Why do we always point at the character of a person just by their history? Why do we not try to find out the details? The reason for a person's action or behaviour? Why do we give a person a media trial without getting down to the bottom of things?"

It felt like her throat was choked. Nayan went to her with a water bottle but she waved him aside and continued.

"As I said my Misty killed her dad. All of you have created an image of her as an evil murderer. Do you even know why she killed him? What was the reason? Let me make one thing clear. If she wouldn't have killed him, I would have for sure."

Everyone started murmuring. She looked back and dragged the man who was being held by her guards. The crowds waited with bated breath to hear what she had to say.

"This man from Africa was here in India to buy my daughter. I am not talking about Misty. Every Indian girl is my daughter, and he chose my blood. Yes, I had planned to kill him because I had got the news and had enough proof. I knew someone from abroad had arrived to get a girl from my state. And I also got proof that it was my ex-husband who had called him. I was in search of the girl they had chosen. But I couldn't find the girl he was going to take to his country. What I had no idea about was that Sameer was about to sell his own daughter to this man whom we caught on his way back to his country."

Maya couldn't control her tears and allowed them to flow for a few seconds.

"Misty did it to save herself from being sold. Misty did it to save your daughters from being sold. Misty did it to teach a lesson to every woman present here. Misty did exactly what I had done. If you could forgive me, why can't you forgive my daughter? The court will decide what should be done with Misty. Thank you."

She folded her hands and raised them above her head and walked through the crowd to her car. The crowd began chanting – 'Justice for Misty' as the car left the hospital.

Police arrested the man and took him with them. The crowd slowly dissipated as I stood there, lost in my thoughts.

Nayan brought me out of my thoughts.

"You and your wife are free now."

"Thanks to Maya, I don't have to be worried about my daughter any longer. We live in a state where Maya rules and justice will prevail."

I smiled and went back to the hospital to be with Mona. I did not need to tell her anything as she had seen everything on TV. She would be released in a few days.

Misty was arrested that day itself. Both husband and wife were locked up in the same jail. In a few days, they were released. Finally, they could live together as a happily married couple. Rajiv's nature changed after the incident. He became calm and responsible.

Misty had become a member of our family now. Her mother never called her again. Maya knew that her daughter was in safe hands.